Broken Promises
Paperback Copyright © 2022 Lorhainne Ekelund
Editor: Talia Leduc

ISBN-13: 9781990590832

Give feedback on the book at:
lorhainneeckhart@hotmail.com

Twitter: @LEckhart
Facebook: AuthorLorhainneEckhart

Printed in the U.S.A

BROKEN PROMISES

The O'Connells

LORHAINNE ECKHART

"I literally could not put this book down once I started reading... absolutely riveting, very thought provoking, and in the end, inspiring."

Rebmay

"Deeply emotional & stirring."

Catlou

"A story telling the whole ugly and corrupt goings on within the justice system."

C. Logue

About the O'Connells

The O'Connells of Livingston, Montana, are not your typical family. Follow them on their journey to the dark and dangerous side of love in a series of romantic thrillers you won't want to miss. Raised by a single mother after their father's mysterious disappearance eighteen years ago, the six grown siblings live in a small town with all kinds of hidden secrets, lies, and deception. Much like the contemporary family romance series focusing on the Friessens, this romantic suspense series follows the lives of the O'Connell family as each of the siblings searches for love.

The O'Connells

The Neighbor
The Third Call
The Secret Husband
The Quiet Day
The Commitment, An O'Connell Novella
The Missing Father
The Hometown Hero
Justice
The Family Secret
The Fallen O'Connell
The Return of the O'Connells
And The She Was Gone
The Stalker
The O'Connell Family Christmas
The Girl Next Door
Broken Promises
The Gatekeeper
The Hunted

She gave her daughter up. Now she wants her back.

What do you do when a woman shows up on your doorstep, suddenly wanting her daughter back? Never in a million years did Marcus and Charlotte O'Connell expect to be faced with this kind of dilemma, but when Reine Colbert is released from prison, she shows up at their house, demanding they return her daughter, Eva.

Worse is the fact that Sheriff Marcus never received a courtesy call from the prison or parole board to warn him that Reine was about to be released. As far as he and Charlotte were concerned, they had followed Reine's wishes, adopting her daughter so she could serve her time, knowing Eva was loved and in a good family. But now she's changed her mind, and she believes Marcus is somehow responsible for her lost years with her daughter.

Though Marcus and his siblings step in to talk it through with Reine, who has been given a raw deal, little Eva is the one caught in the middle of the tug of war.

Will the O'Connells be able to reason with a woman who has no reason to trust anyone? Find out in a novel about secrets, hurts, lies, and the true of meaning of family.

Chapter One

___

S he was thirty-one years old, and she had a daughter, a tattoo she would never be able to remove, eighteen dollars and forty cents in her pocket, and a prison record that would keep her from ever having anything else. Reine Colbert wondered when she hadn't felt this hollow ache that had become a part of her, of who she was, an anger that had only grown deeper, so much that it burned her with every breath she took.

She stared at the brick homes, sidewalks, and grass lawns of picture-perfect suburbia, with flowers planted in front of porches that welcomed visitors, family, and friends with glasses of lemonade, laughter, and small talk.

But that life wasn't for someone like her. That life had been ripped from her. Reine had once had a husband, a daughter. She'd once felt joy. Now she felt only anger.

It hurt more than anything to feel she was supposed to be thankful that she got to breathe the same air as people who had homes, lives, and freedom. Wasn't that exactly what her parole officer had said after he finished grinding her into the ground as she sat in his dingy office, realizing he didn't see her as human? He'd stared at her file instead of her, making it clear she'd never matter. She'd better learn her place, keep her nose clean, take what was offered. And he didn't want to hear any complaints or whining about anything, because rights were something she didn't have.

No drugs, no liquor, no weapons.

And the last, which had nearly choked her, was *no respect.* That was something she wasn't entitled to anymore. She'd been officially categorized as a person with no rights and no dignity, and she was terrified, as she stood on the concrete sidewalk, seeing weeds sprouting up between the cracks here and there, staring at a house, that what she was doing now could have her right back behind bars.

It would take just one call from someone who mattered, even though that would be cruel. Then again, cruelty had become familiar to her, and it was a quality she saw in everyone now.

Someone was watching her. This was that feeling prison had taught her, the one that had kept her alive and breathing. She waited a second before turning to see a woman with long dark hair across the street, staring.

Reine pulled at her old hoodie, lifting the hood over her shoulder-length dark hair even though it was mildly warm out. She made herself look away, around and up the street to see what could be coming at her. It was a quiet morning, and cars were parked in front of most of the houses. The sheriff's cruiser was in the driveway as the early sun topped the horizon.

She reminded herself she couldn't keep standing there, as someone would call the cops, and she'd be questioned, told she didn't belong. Reine made herself take one step and then another, hoping whoever was watching her would let her be instead of hitting her with the knowledge that she didn't belong there.

She kept moving in sneakers that were so worn she could feel each pebble she stepped on, but the pain was welcome as she walked up the sidewalk toward the two-story craftsman. Her legs were shaking, and her stomach was hollow, and Reine was very aware of the voices she could hear from inside.

The three front steps were painted gray. As she stepped up, she glanced down at the holes in her sneakers, and her heartbeat thudded long and loud in her ears. The hair on the back of her neck stood up. She wondered whether she'd ever shake that feeling of being watched, having to look over her shoulder, never feeling a moment's peace because of that deep ache in her soul, a reminder of everything she'd lost.

She took another step up, and the creak of the wood ricocheted through her. Her inhale was long and loud in her ears, her heart pounding, her hands sweating. One more step, and she knew she shouldn't be here, fearing the hand that would reach for her and pull her back, another living nightmare. Reine prayed for the day when that fear would truly leave her.

She fisted her shaking hand, feeling the sweat under her arms, down her back. Her blue jeans hung on her hips. The inside door was closed, and she stared at the screen mesh and lifted her hand to ring the doorbell, but instead she knocked on the white painted frame.

The sound was weak. Standing there, she wasn't sure

if anyone had heard her. She lifted her hand again when she heard voices and footsteps, and then the door opened. She'd never forget his face, his blue eyes, that all-cop look, even though she'd forgotten how tall he was, standing there in his sheriff's uniform.

For a moment, the silence hung thick in the air as she stared at the man who was responsible for everything she didn't have.

"Marcus, who's at the door?" someone called out. It was her voice, Charlotte.

Reine fisted her hands where they hung at her sides and stared through the screen that separated her from a man she felt only bitterness for. She took in the confusion that knit his brows, his hand on the door. He didn't answer his wife.

"Reine?"

Was he happy or angry? She couldn't tell from his deep voice. The screen was still closed, but then he pushed it open with a loud squeak. She heard the sounds of children and a voice she'd go to her grave knowing, because it was a part of her.

Eva.

"I don't understand. What…? How?" Marcus gestured toward her, and she could hear the confusion as his gaze bore down on her. "What are you doing here?"

She pulled her hood down. "Hello, Marcus," she said, her heart still hammering as she took in the gun holstered on his duty belt. Once, she'd never have believed she could come to hate that uniform, but now she did because of what it had taken from her.

He was still standing in the doorway, looking down at her. She knew she wouldn't be invited in. What, exactly, had she expected?

"Marcus, you didn't answer. Who's here…?" There she was, Charlotte, dressed for work in a brown deputy's shirt, her long dark hair pulled up. Her eyes widened as she stood beside Marcus, staring down at her. Charlotte's head just topped his shoulders, but they were both taller than her.

She was still trembling inside, facing the gatekeepers to her Eva. More guards, even though she was no longer behind the walls of a prison.

"Reine, what are you doing here?" Charlotte said. "I didn't know you were out. What's going on?"

Not even a welcome or a smile. That was something she expected, and there it was, the change in Charlotte's face, in her eyes. Gone was the caring, and the woman who'd taken her daughter was staring at her now in a way that told her she didn't want her here.

"I'm here to see my daughter," Reine said.

She didn't miss the exchange between husband and wife as if her fate was still up for debate, as if someone else decided what she could and couldn't do.

"You're out of prison?" Marcus said. "I don't understand. When did this happen?"

When had she become so aware of the tone of people's voices? Marcus's had an edge she hadn't expected.

"Yes, I'm out. I hope that's not a problem for you." She wondered if sarcasm dripped from her words. Maybe that was why she still hadn't been invited in.

Marcus stepped out of the house, forcing her to take a step back, something she was too familiar with. Then he took another and another, and she had to fight the urge to look back to see the steps she could fall down. He was right in front of her, his hands on his duty belt beside cuffs she hoped never to feel around her wrists again. But she refused to cower even though she was terrified of what he could do to her.

The screen door hadn't closed, and she knew Charlotte was still standing there, holding it open.

"Marcus, the children…"

Was that worry or fear in Charlotte's voice? Reine couldn't look at her because the sheriff was staring down at her with a hard expression, the only way people looked at her now.

"Go inside and take Eva and Cameron upstairs," he said without pulling his eyes from her.

Reine wasn't about to lower her gaze, either, even though looking a guard in the eye in prison would have been seen as challenging, threatening, with repercussions that ranged from having her privileges taken away to being beaten or tossed in isolation. Cruel was cruel, and that had been all she'd known for too long.

Reine made herself take a breath and instinctively fisted her hands at her sides again.

"Marcus, everything okay here? Jenny said there may be something wrong," came a voice from behind her.

She had to look away, down to the man looking up at her from the sidewalk in a park warden's uniform. He was tall, too, and from the way he looked at her, she could feel this going sideways.

"No, everything is fine, Ryan," Marcus said. "This is Reine. She's out of prison." He sounded so matter of fact, but the way he talked about her, as if addressing the weather or the news, ached.

From how the other man was looking at her now, she expected to be told to leave or maybe walked down the street by the two of them, out of the neighborhood, with a warning never to come back.

"You have my daughter, Marcus," she said. "I want to see Eva right now."

He lifted his gaze back to her sharply with an expression she didn't like, shaking his head. "I don't think that's a good idea, Reine. She's happy now, and she wouldn't understand. You just showing up here like this isn't good for her. It's confusing, and—"

"She's my daughter!" She thumped her chest with her fisted hand, cutting him off, and it felt so damn good to do it, because it was something she'd never have been allowed to do in prison.

His gaze snapped to the sudden movement, and she reminded herself she was in front of a cop, standing right on his doorstep. She needed to be careful not to be construed as threatening or aggressive, even though the words she wanted to say were screaming through her head. The anger that radiated through her was clouding her reasoning.

"No, Reine," Marcus said. "She's our daughter now. Charlotte and I adopted her. Did you forget it was your idea? Now you're showing up here without calling, demanding to see her. What is this?"

That was something else she'd become far too used to, being denied everything she loved. The lump in her throat threatened to choke her, and tears burned her eyes from the anger that was only swelling deeper, bigger, burning a hole right through her.

"This is about my daughter, Marcus. Mine. I gave birth to her, and she was taken from me…"

He lifted a hand, and for a moment she thought he would touch her, so she jerked her shoulder sharply away. He must have known, as he pulled his hand back. "I can see you're angry and hurt, but I really don't think right now is a good time," he said. "We'll talk, and maybe we can look at something down the road when you're a little more settled." His hand went to his duty belt again, and she felt the dismissal, knowing the other man was still standing there, watching her, maybe waiting for her to move too fast or do something he didn't like.

Reine didn't nod. This was too familiar, being told to leave. Then they'd circle the wagons and make sure Eva was moved further out of reach. She was shaking her head as she said, "No, I'm not leaving. I came to see my daughter, and you can't keep her from me."

"Reine, you're making this very difficult. I said no. What is it you really want here? What is this really about? If you were truly thinking of Eva's best interest, you wouldn't be here now, showing up without calling."

She tried to look past him, but he was right there, blocking the door. She lifted her chin and refused to look away from the hard blue eyes of the cop looking down on her. "What I really want is to have the life that was stolen from me. That's what I really want, Marcus. But I can't have that, and I have to live with the shitty hand I was dealt. I've already asked you, and you've denied me seeing my daughter. So hear me, Marcus O'Connell. I'm standing here on your doorstep, and you have my daughter inside, and I'm telling you I want her back. Not to visit, not to make an appointment so you can decide whether I can or can't see her. I want her back. She's mine." She was trembling and knew she should be terrified by the way he was staring down at her.

"No, absolutely not," he snapped.

She picked up the sharp edge in his voice and heard the creak of the step behind her, knowing her time was up. A hand would grab her and push her away.

She didn't think. She could feel the panic and the agony of her daughter being ripped away from her again. It was her sweet face, her image, and her name that had kept her sane, so she did the only thing she could think of. She opened her mouth and yelled, "Eva!"

Chapter Two

"What do you want to do?"

Marcus leaned on the island, pressing his hands against the edge of the laminate as he listened to his daughter, Eva, talking to a woman he couldn't believe had shown up at his door. He looked at Charlotte, whose brown eyes seemed to darken with a worry he'd never seen before. As she ran her hand over his arm, he only shrugged and shook his head, then pushed away from the island. "I don't know. I can't believe I didn't get a call that she was getting out, even just as a courtesy. Our office should have been notified. I'll find out who her parole officer is and have a word with him."

Charlotte touched his arm again. "What about work? We have to go. We were supposed to be there already, but we can't leave her here. Eva has school, too. She's already late. I can't believe Reine called out for her like she did. You should have seen Eva's face when she heard Reine. The way she yelled, I couldn't stop her from running down the stairs."

He shut his eyes, feeling the ache, wondering whether he'd ever shake the moment when he heard the desperation in Reine's cry for Eva. It had cut him deep inside, and so had the footsteps of the little girl he loved so much on the stairs, her face as she pushed open that screen door, and her voice as she cried out, "Mommy!"

The entire situation had spiraled out of his control.

He only nodded and slid his hand over his wife's arm, feeling how tense she was.

"You want me to walk in there and ask her to leave?" she said.

He shook his head. "I can't do that to Eva. Let her have a minute with Reine to talk, but I think you should go to work. Jenny good to keep Cameron?"

His wife made a face and sighed. He was grateful that Ryan had at least taken Cameron back to his house and out of the emotion of Reine having just shown up. He still hadn't told Charlotte what she'd said.

"Yeah, of course," Charlotte replied. "She called your mom, too. At least Iris won't be sitting there, waiting for Cameron to show up. I have to get Eva to school."

He heard the squeak of the front door and footsteps, and he lifted his gaze to his brother Ryan as he walked in. Ryan gestured with his thumb to the living room, where mother and daughter were sitting. The expression on his face said everything.

"So what's the plan here, Marcus?" Ryan said. "She staying for the day? She really planning on taking Eva back?"

Charlotte hissed beside him. "She wants Eva back?"

"Shh," he said, taking a step and sliding both his

hands over Charlotte's shoulders, the only way he could think to keep her from running into the living room and pulling Eva, the little girl who was their daughter, away from Reine. "Keep your voice down."

Charlotte's face paled. He hadn't expected it to come out so sharply.

"She said she wants her daughter back," he said, "but I haven't had a chance to talk to her. We're running completely on emotion here…"

When he let his hands fall away, Charlotte moved to step back, so he touched her arm again and said, "No, don't you go in there and make this worse. I can see your anger, but going in there now will only further complicate this situation we find ourselves in. Remember, we adopted Eva officially. She can't just walk in and take her."

Marcus slipped his hand around Charlotte's arm and gave her a little tug, feeling the war raging inside her. She only wanted to protect Eva.

Ryan was quiet, watching them. Just as Marcus realized he couldn't hear Eva and Reine talking anymore, he heard the creak of the floorboards and turned to see them stepping quietly into the kitchen.

"Hey, there," Marcus said, resting his hand on the edge of the island beside him and doing his best to keep his voice light. "You're supposed to be at school. We have to get going soon."

Eva was holding Reine's hand, and he took in the way she looked up to her mother, seeing how hesitant and thrown his little girl had to be. "I don't want to go to school today. Can't I stay here with Mommy?" she said, her voice no longer that of the confident little girl who had settled in with them.

He knew Charlotte couldn't pull her gaze from how tightly Reine gripped Eva's hand. Her clothes were worn and old. He couldn't remember whether those were the ones she'd been arrested in. He had so many damn questions, and he could see panic staring back at him from the face of a little girl who'd had her life turned upside down.

"Eva, you love school," Charlotte said, slipping away from him to squat down in front of Eva and reach out for her. "This was just a short visit with Reine this morning. You'll see her again. We'll have her over. Come on, you go and get your shoes on. This isn't goodbye. Come on." She slid her hand over Eva's arm, rubbing it.

Eva looked up to Reine, who was still holding her other hand, as if waiting for her mother to say it was okay. He couldn't have this, so he took a step toward them, seeing the determination on Reine's face. From her silence and the way she stared back at him with a hard, unforgiving look, it was clear she had no intention of letting go of Eva's hand. He wondered whether she expected to walk out of the house with his daughter. He needed to remind her it didn't work like that.

"Charlotte's right, Eva," he said. "We'll have Reine over, but you need to go get your shoes on, and Charlotte will take you to school. Remember, Grandma is picking you up today, and it's family night at her house tonight. Right now, Reine and I need to talk. Isn't that right, Reine?"

When he lifted his gaze to her, Reine was staring at him with a hate he'd never expected. It made absolutely no sense, and he was so damn furious at this situation.

"Can Mommy stay, Marcus?" Eva said. "I don't want to go to school today…"

He shook his head. "Hey, don't worry. You'll see her again."

"Can she come to Grandma's tonight, to family night? You have to come, Mommy, please. Uncle Owen always barbecues, and Uncle Luke and Chloe have a dog they always bring…" Eva was looking from Charlotte, to him, to her mother, and he could see the hope he couldn't take from her.

"Eva, if Reine doesn't have plans already, of course she can come," he said, "but Reine and I need to talk, and you need to go to school. Go get your shoes on and say goodbye to Reine." He took one step closer and then another, dragging his gaze to Reine. She had to know she was pushing him, and maybe that was why she made a face, squeezed Eva's hand, and leaned down to her.

"Marcus is right," she said, "but I'll see you tonight. I promise I will be there. No one will keep me from being there." Reine lifted her hard gaze to him as she spoke, and he could already feel the fight building in her.

She ran her hand over Eva's head before kissing her forehead, and as she let her hand go, Marcus let out the breath he hadn't known he was holding. He realized then how tight his chest was, and the relief he blew out was louder than expected.

Charlotte was right behind Eva. He knew she'd have her out the door and in her car quickly by the way she was urging her to get her shoes on. Reine turned, facing the door, her arms across her stomach, and he already saw her anger toward him. This conversation would be anything but friendly.

"Marcus, Eva's lunch," Charlotte called out.

He pulled open the fridge and reached for the paper bag in which Charlotte had packed Eva's favorite, a cheese and lettuce sandwich, along with a fruit cup, a bag of carrots (the only vegetable she'd eat), and a cookie from the chocolate chip batch Charlotte had baked for the kids. He rolled up the edge of the paper bag.

"Okay, I see you got the last chocolate chip cookie again," he said, forcing the teasing back into his voice as he walked around Reine and Ryan, who leaned against the island without saying a word. He kept going, one step and then another, seeing the panic and uncertainty flickering in Eva's innocent blue eyes. They weren't the O'Connell blue but a different shade, Reine's shade, yet without the same disillusionment and rage at the weight of the world.

He made himself blow out a breath as he stood over Eva, who was sitting on the steps, and Charlotte, who was helping her lace up her shoes. That was something he hadn't seen her do for Eva in a long time. Marcus held out the paper lunch bag. "So when you're eating that cookie today, think of me watching you and knowing you got the last one."

She took the paper bag, and there was the hint of a smile. "We'll make some more. Maybe Mommy could help," she said with a hopeful look to Charlotte, who stood abruptly.

"Okay, we have to go, Eva," she said, an edge to her voice. "Say goodbye to Reine."

Eva left the lunch bag on the steps and ran back to the kitchen. Marcus leaned on the wooden railing of the staircase, watching as she hugged Reine, who was on her knees, holding her daughter so tight. He couldn't make out what she whispered to her before she kissed her again.

Marcus dragged his hand over his face, hearing the scrape of whiskers even though he'd shaved, and then shook his head as he saw the panic in his wife's face. She had her purse and the lunch bag as she waited. Finally, Reine let Eva go, and Eva ran over to Charlotte with a big bright smile.

After Charlotte had her out the door, the silence lingered, and he could've sworn he heard the tick of a clock from someplace in the house. He listened to Charlotte's Subaru starting up before dragging his gaze back to a woman who had suddenly turned their morning upside down. His brother was still standing behind her, and Reine stared at him too with the kind of anger he'd seen too many times on the faces of people he'd arrested. Being a cop, he had grown far too used to seeing that.

He pushed away from the dark wood of the rail, noting how tense she was. "I know Eva invited you to my mother's tonight, but I don't want you there. We have some things to settle first, some ground rules to lay out. For one, you coming in here and threatening to take that little girl from us… It isn't going to happen. Did you forget we adopted her? You signed over your parental rights. It's too late, Reine. There is no going back." He was shaking his head, stepping toward her.

She tracked each of his movements, and he wondered whether it was fear he was seeing now instead of the rage he'd first thought. "Well, that's where you're wrong, Marcus O'Connell. She's my daughter, and I was left with little choice. I will have it reversed, and I'm taking my daughter. You can fight me and try to keep me away, but if you do that, Eva will hate you."

She wasn't cowering. He knew when someone was bluffing, and this was a woman who wasn't going to quietly walk away.

"Do you think I'm just going to let you walk in here and rip her world apart, and ours?" he said. "No, she's our daughter now. We love her—"

"No, she's my daughter." Reine cut him off and slapped her hand sharply to her chest. "And you are not keeping me from her. Do not come any closer to me, Marcus."

He stopped, watching the heave of her chest.

Ryan was watching her, too. "You know what? This isn't getting us anywhere," he finally said, stepping in, staring down at Reine. Then he dragged his gaze over to Marcus. "You need to get going, Marcus. Go on. Reine, you, Charlotte, and Marcus really need to sit down and talk, but now isn't a good time. It'd be better if your heads were cooler."

The last thing Marcus wanted was to walk out of his house without setting some ground rules with Reine, but Ryan took another step and got right in front of him, saying in a low voice, "Go. You're only butting heads. There's no reasoning right now. Go to work. I've got this."

He didn't want to agree.

Maybe that was why his brother angled his head and glanced back to Reine, asking, "You had breakfast yet?"

She didn't say anything, just shook her head.

Marcus realized maybe his brother was right. "You call me later," was all he said to Ryan before taking a step away.

"Yeah, later," Ryan replied.

Marcus kept right on going to the door, where he set his hand on the screen and stood for a second, watching Reine watching him. Ryan was waiting, and he didn't have a clue how to reason with this woman.

Chapter Three

Charlotte was perched on the edge of his desk, where he sat with the phone to his ear, the door closed. He'd said nothing to Therese and Colby about his personal business, and then there was Harold, who he knew was handling a call at a property north of town about vandalized farm equipment and a fire that had destroyed half a barn. Arson for sure, but not something he could get his head into today.

He listened to the ring again, furious after having left two messages for the warden of the women's prison, who had never bothered to call him back.

"Jane Bartlett," she finally answered, and the ball of rage building in his stomach seemed to grow bigger.

"Warden Bartlett, this is Sheriff Marcus O'Connell. You're a hard woman to get a hold of. Pretty sure I left two messages for you already."

"Sheriff, I'm busy running a prison. What can I do for you?" she said sharply. He still remembered how she'd laid the law down on him when Reine was locked up, calling that prison home for nearly three years. Her words, exactly, had been *Stay the hell out of how I run my prison.*

"I'm calling about Reine Colbert. I would have expected a courtesy call from you to say she was being released."

There was no pause on the other end, no *Oops, sorry.* "Why would I notify you? Her lawyer managed to get her before the parole board, and she was granted early release. Is there a problem I should know about? Because unless she's done something and is having her parole revoked and being returned to my prison, I'm not clear on why we should be talking. The last thing I have any time for is to notify people when a prisoner is being released. As far as I'm concerned, she's done her time. All she has to do is keep her nose clean. If she gets herself in trouble, she'll land right back here and will have to serve out the remainder of her sentence. Again, did she do something? Otherwise, I don't want to hear about it."

Sometimes he appreciated when a woman got to the point, but right now, the way she talked to him was only pissing him off. Worse, he expected her to cut him off and hang up. Charlotte didn't pull her gaze from him until he heard a knock on his door, when she slid off the desk and walked over to pull it open.

He looked away, turning his chair toward the large framed map of Montana on the dark wood wall, and shut his eyes for a second, then dragged his hand down over his face, knowing everything would go sideways with this warden when he opened his mouth.

"Look, she showed up at my door this morning," he said. "I would have appreciated a heads-up so I could prepare and have an idea—"

The warden sighed. "So you've arrested her."

He hadn't expected that. He realized the warden likely didn't remember about her daughter, and he found himself shaking his head. "No, of course I didn't. My wife and I adopted Reine's daughter, Eva…"

"Of course, yes." She cut him off. "Well, I'm sure her parole officer will have already advised her not to contact you and her daughter. So she couldn't help herself. Seems too often they're out and then right back in here. Okay, here it is. Manny Meskill is her parole officer. You want the number?"

There was something odd about the warden. He never knew what side of the fence she was on.

"No, I know Manny," he said, recalling a man in his fifties, five inches shorter than Marcus, with messy dark hair, a penchant for fast food, and a belly that hung over his belt. "I'll call him."

"Is there anything else, Sheriff?" There it was, the unfriendliness back in her tone as if she didn't want to hear from him again.

"No, I'll have a word with Manny. Thank you, Warden."

He heard the click and knew she'd hung up, so he set the phone back in the cradle with a clatter and slid his office chair around. It squeaked as he leaned forward, resting his forearms on his desk, seeing Harold in the doorway. Evidently, Charlotte was bringing him up to speed. The door was wide open as she walked back over to him.

"Well, what did she say?"

Marcus reached for the phone again to call Manny, a man he'd talked to half a dozen times, but then decided against it. He let out a heavy sigh, feeling Charlotte staring down at him, waiting for him to answer as he tried to wrap his head around this situation.

"Manny Meskill is her parole officer. Her lawyer got her early parole. Karen should have called me and told me…"

"Maybe your sister didn't know," Charlotte said.

Harold stared at them, just taking it all in, standing right in front of his desk beside her. "Karen did say sometime about Reine's father, Duncan, bringing in his own lawyer. Wasn't he handling things for her now? You know we were cut out of the loop."

Marcus needed to call his sister. "I'll call Karen, see what she can find out. In the meantime, I'll have a word with the parole officer."

He didn't have a clue how to deal with Reine's anger, and he hadn't really taken the time to consider what would happen when she got out, what it would mean for her to eventually walk through the doors of the prison. It shouldn't have happened so early, but evidently, here they were.

"She threaten you?" Harold said, resting his hands on his duty belt, all cop, staring down at him.

Charlotte's gaze lingered on him. Wouldn't it be so easy to say she had?

He made himself shake his head. He could see the panic in Charlotte's gaze. She expected him to figure out how to keep Reine away. "No, she didn't threaten me or us. I wouldn't say that about her. She wants Eva back, though, which has me wondering what else is coming our way. She's angry, and the way she showed up, I'm not sure what she'll do. A woman on the edge, operating on pure emotion… It's not an ideal situation, and it's not exactly what I want around my daughter."

Harold dragged his gaze from Charlotte to him, taking it all in.

"So was it arson?" Marcus changed the subject because he needed to think of something else for a moment so he could be reasonable instead of reverting to the hard-ass he likely had been that morning.

Harold shook his head. "Looks like it. Tracking down a couple leads, but seems it could be the same person who wrecked the farm equipment and cut fencing at those two other properties, the Olsons' place and Lloyd Binnion's down the road."

Marcus reached for the keys on his desk and his cell phone, shoving them in his pocket as he stood up, knowing Charlotte still expected him to do something. "You got this, then?" He gestured to Harold, who just lifted his hands.

"Yeah, I got it. What are you planning on doing? Charlotte said you left your house and Ryan was there with Reine. What happened?"

Another call he needed to make. This was his problem, but Ryan had obviously picked up on how sideways it was going.

He took in the open door, unable to shake that off feeling he had, and gestured helplessly, dragging his gaze back over to Charlotte, his wife, the mother of his children, Eva and Cameron. "Maybe Ryan got through to her. I expected him to call. Eva wants Reine to come to family night at Mom's."

Harold opened his mouth the way he did when he didn't know what to say.

Marcus dragged his gaze back over to Charlotte, who crossed her arms over her chest, her lips pressed tightly in a fine line. "I told her no after you left, told her she can't come," he said. "So that's where it was left. Right now, I'm going to pay Manny Meskill a visit and find out why he couldn't pick up the damn phone and give me a call. He should've let me know Reine was out so I could do damage control and figure out a few things instead of being blindsided completely this morning when she showed up at our door. Then I'm going to find out where she's staying, everything he said to her, and where the fuck she got this idea that she can just walk out of prison and take Eva back. Eva is ours now. I'll have that chat with Manny, see that things are squared away and he sits down with Reine so she gets her head on straight…"

"Marcus, you mind some advice?" Harold cut in, which was something he didn't normally do. But then, Marcus couldn't remember the last time he'd gone so far off the rails. He wanted to say no, as he could see Charlotte expected him to just handle this. He let out a heavy sigh as he held the keys.

"Sure, why not?" He could feel the sarcasm dripping from his tone, but Harold didn't seem to notice.

"Maybe you need to sit down with Reine and just listen to her," he said, then lifted his hands as if he'd overstepped, likely because Marcus could feel the *Hell, no!* on the tip of his tongue. "Look, just hear me out here. What is it you're planning on doing? You're going to see Manny and, what, have her parole yanked and get her tossed back in jail? You want to make her life more difficult than it already is?"

Marcus pulled his hand over his face. He wasn't that kind of cop, he was better than that, but this was his daughter, Eva. "I don't know. No… I'm not out to toss her back in jail, but the entire situation of her being there wasn't right. Nevertheless, this is where we are, and the fact is she's messing with my family. She's going to hurt Eva, and I can't have that."

Charlotte still hadn't said anything. She was looking at the door, and he knew she wanted to race out of there, pick up Eva from school, pick up Cameron from Jenny's, and lock the doors at home and not let them out.

"Hey, I get it," Harold said. "I can see how wound tight you both are. But don't forget she's Eva's mother, so tread carefully. Eva is old enough to understand that her mother showed up this morning, so if she doesn't see her again, she's going to ask why. Are you going to lie to her or say it's complicated? Because I have to tell you, that kid is smart, and if she figures it out or finds out you did something…"

How the hell did Harold do that? His words of reason were an icy splash of water

"Shit! Fuck…" Marcus said. "God almighty, she'd never forgive us." He dragged his hand over his face again and turned back to the map on the wall, wondering why he was so damn focused on it. Then he made himself look back to Harold, who made a face and angled his head, pulling his arms across his chest.

"Again, Marcus, talk to her, sit down with her, find some common ground. Because I can see already what this is going to do. From where I'm standing, it could tear you apart, and that happy little girl. Anger is anger. Reine evidently wants to be part of her life. Can you really deny her that, or Eva?"

He pressed his hand over his eyes. Harold's words of wisdom told him something he already knew deep down. He tucked his phone in his pocket.

"I'm still having a talk with Manny," was all he said, then started around his desk, feeling the reality of the situation. When he reached the doorway, he turned back, carrying the weight of every moment of what had happened to Reine: her survival, her wrong choices, her ending up on the wrong end of the law. "I'm just talking, that's it. I'm not heading there to cause Reine trouble."

But he still planned on talking one on one with Reine, too. And this time, he hoped the woman he spoke to was the same reasonable one who'd asked him to adopt Eva.

Chapter Four

"Mrs. Hirst, is there anything else I can get for you before I go? Now, Reine is going to finish up here, and then your daughter will be back, so if you need anything, just call for Reine and she can get it for you."

Reine couldn't hear how the old woman answered Ivy Smoat, the homecare nurse for whom Reine did all the grunt work. As she wiped the bathtub down, she remembered how the O'Connells had looked down on her and the agony of not being able to be a mother to her daughter.

She took in the floor she still needed to clean and the bed she needed to change. Should she say something about the fact that the old woman was soiling the bed again? Reine had found the adult diapers she was supposedly wearing tucked in the oddest of places. The daughter had to have noticed. But then, she remembered how she'd raced out of the house for a hair appointment or massage—she couldn't remember which—as soon as they arrived.

"Hey, when you're done there I need you to run upstairs and tidy up," Ivy told her. "Run the vacuum, clean the bathrooms, and do Valerie's room, too. She's got a lot on her plate, looking after her mom." She made a motion of looking at her watch. "Now, Valerie said she'd be back around two."

She stood in the doorway, a big woman who had five inches and a hundred pounds on Reine. She had a dark round face and eyes that said she didn't care or want to hear anything about Reine's problems or her business. She wondered if that was why it always felt as if Ivy were talking down to her.

Reine squeezed her fist, holding the sponge on her knees by the bathtub, wondering whether she should point out that homecare meant looking after the old woman, not her daughter, and she worked only until one thirty. But instead she just shrugged and said, "Sure."

Ivy let her gaze linger a second, and Reine felt the knot in her stomach. Had she said it the wrong way? She wondered why the woman was still staring down at her. She knew well when someone still had something to say, and the only thing she expected was something else to grind her down.

"I wasn't going to say anything," Ivy said, "but you were late this morning. Showing up all sweaty, running in the way you did as I was loading up the car, I can't have that happening again, do you hear? And since you were assigned to me, to help me, I expect reliability. Tomorrow, make sure you show up to help me get the supplies before we leave for the homes we're visiting. You'll have to walk back to the office today. I have to leave now and get over to the Johnsons', so when you're done, just leave the bucket and cleaning supplies downstairs. Reine, consider this the only warning I'll give you. Plan on being at the office fifteen minutes early, because that's what the boss likes to see. I don't want to be in that position of wondering whether you'll even show, because if you don't, you won't have a job. You understand?"

She wanted to argue, to explain how she'd had to run sixteen blocks from the O'Connells' because she'd needed to see her daughter. Even though she knew Ryan had wanted a word with her, she'd run out the door right after Marcus pulled away. Probably not something she should mention. Going toe to toe with Marcus O'Connell hadn't been what she'd planned to do—not yet, anyway. Then there was his family.

"I'm sorry. It won't happen again," she said.

Ivy didn't smile except when she was sitting and talking with the old woman. "Well, we'll see, won't we?" she said with a bite.

Reine realized she'd found herself on the bad side of her supervisor, but then, she wondered whether Ivy had made up her mind about her from the moment Reine was assigned to her. She'd come with the label of ex-con, out on probation. Her anxiety only twisted tighter in her stomach.

"We have three calls on the schedule tomorrow, and you have to wear the company scrubs, as is outlined in the employee handbook," Ivy said.

Reine didn't bother to get up. Should she point out that she was supposed to leave with Ivy? She was just the homecare assistant. She was to arrive and leave with the homecare nurse and do everything she asked. Also, although she was four days on the job now, she'd been told they didn't have the uniform in her size.

"Sorry, Ivy, but I asked again yesterday about the scrubs and was told my size was backordered. Not sure what you want me to do."

Ivy flicked her gaze down to her and gave her head a shake. "Well, then you should pick up something else to wear in the meantime instead of those ripped blue jeans. It's not a good image for the company. Because I'm not completely heartless, I realize you've likely not had time to shop. There is a secondhand store on Third that might have something that would work."

Reine squeezed the sponge, still remembering her parole officer tossing her the name and number for Better Way Homecare, saying it would be a dream job for her. "I'm doing the best I can, Ivy, but I haven't even been paid my first check. This is all I have. Secondhand store or not, it's going to cost money," she said, but as soon as it was out of her mouth, she realized she should've said nothing. "You know what? I'll figure something out."

Apparently, that was what Ivy wanted to hear, by the way she gave her a nod and stared down at her. "You do that, then," she said, then moved to step away.

"Oh, just to clarify, you're leaving me alone to finish, and you don't need help at the Johnsons'?"

Ivy gripped the strap of her black purse and pulled her keys from her pocket. "No, I don't need help at the Johnsons' until Friday, because that's when he's on the schedule for a longer visit, with a bath and a big clean of the house. Today, I just need to check his sugar levels, make sure he's taken his insulin. I figure I'll be in and out in five minutes, ten tops. Friday will be the cleaning and everything else, so plan on being there most of the day. Oh, and I forgot to mention the fridge here. Clean it out if you get a chance. I noticed a lot of old uncovered food. Just toss it all."

Apparently, this was the "everything else" she was supposed to be doing.

"What if I run out of time? I'm supposed to be off in an hour…" She stopped talking, because from the way Ivy let her gaze linger on her again, she knew she was going to have to do more and talk less.

"Are we going to have a problem here?" Ivy said.

Reine made herself close her mouth and shook her head.

"We're taking a chance on you, Reine. We don't normally hire ex-cons. Should I be worried about leaving you here to finish?"

What the hell was she supposed to say to that? It was a familiar reminder that she had to know her place. "Dehumanization" was a word that cut so deeply in her soul, a word she'd heard too often from the lips of other inmates, and now that was all she felt.

"Of course not," Reine said. "Just wanted to be clear on the rules. See you tomorrow?" She forced a smile to her lips even though she felt this going sideways. That had been her life for too long.

"Again, don't be late tomorrow. And talk to Pete when you get back to the office about the uniform. Wear something that at least looks like scrubs. Pete is really big on all us girls looking the part."

Then she was gone, and Reine let out a sigh, falling back on her heels and hearing the outside door close. She pictured her daughter's face again and imagined the talk she hadn't had with Ryan. She knew she didn't want to hear him warn her off.

But at least she wasn't locked in a cage, with people

telling her when she had to go to bed, when she had to get up. She had no intention of ever going back again. Now she was on the outside, having to visit a man who could make her life a living hell.

She was taking a second to remember her daughter, just sitting with her that morning while she fought the giant ache of the years she'd lost with her, when she heard a crash from what sounded like the kitchen. She dropped the sponge in the bathtub, yanked off the rubber gloves, and ran out of the bathroom to see the woman, who she knew was in her seventies, standing over a broken clay plant pot. Dirt was spilled everywhere, and she was standing right in the middle of a pile of it.

"Oh no, Mrs. Hirst..." she started, seeing how confused the woman was. "Come on, careful now, watch your step." She put her hand on the old woman, taking in the navy polyester slacks, the loose blue and white top, her hair still damp from the bath she'd just had.

"Oh dear, what did I do?"

"Were you trying to water the plant, Mrs. Hirst?" Reine helped her take a step back—in her slippers, thankfully.

"I don't know," she said, still confused.

How was she supposed to clean and keep this old woman out of trouble? She helped her into the living room, back to her chair.

"I'll check the plants for you," Reine said. "You sit back here by the window and see what a nice pretty day it is. Can I get you some water?" There was a mug of coffee there, still full, and a small wooden box on top of a newspaper, as well as a book she didn't think she'd read.

"Who are you?"

"I'm Reine, remember? I came with Ivy."

Mrs. Hirst reached over to the box and opened the lid to pull out a pearl necklace that was tangled with a bunch of other earrings and necklaces. "Could you help me put this on?"

"Of course I can." Reine took the pearl necklace from her shaking hands and opened the clasp, then put it on her, wondering if this was what the old woman had to look forward to. "There, that looks so nice."

The woman touched the pearls. "Herman gave me these on our first anniversary."

She could see the old woman had evidently been pulled into a fond memory. "Who is Herman, your husband?"

Mrs. Hirst looked up to her again. "Who are you?"

Reine realized this was going to be a really long day. "I'm Reine. So, Mrs. Hirst, I need you to stay here. I'm going to clean up the mess in the kitchen."

Reine took in the clock as she strode back into the kitchen, spotting a broom tucked in the corner. She realized she would be here longer than she wanted. As she swept up the dirt, she heard a creak and footsteps, and she glanced up to see Mrs. Hirst walking down the hall. She wanted to scream. Cleaning was one thing, but looking after a woman struggling with dementia was far outside her comfort zone and not what she'd signed up for.

"Mrs. Hirst, where are you going?" she called out.

Then the old woman walked back down the hall, now wearing a robe, and went right to the front door and opened it.

Chapter Five

Marcus's phone was ringing. He took in the caller ID, Karen Curtis, and wondered when his sister had taken her husband's name.

"So you're finally calling me back. Took you long enough," he said as he pulled up in front of the old commercial building where Reine's parole officer, Manny Meskill, had his office. He put the car in park and turned it off before pulling the keys from the ignition, hearing Charlotte's voice over his radio, then Harold's, about a call in progress and a wellness check on some old-timer.

"Oh, park the nasty, already, Marcus. I was in a meeting. So what's up with you? You said something in your message about Reine Colbert? And, just FYI, my husband—you know, the governor? Well, his assistant was in my office when I played your message out loud."

He couldn't remember what he'd said, exactly, when he was sent right to voicemail, other than *Pick up the damn phone!* or something along those lines. He shook his head as he sat in his parked car, staring at the dingy glass front that led to a narrow hallway. He knew the parole officer's office was in back, with hard wooden benches in the hall where the parolees would sit and wait.

"Reine Colbert showed up at my door this morning, demanding to see Eva," he said. "It was not a good scene. I tried to get her to leave, but everything went sideways when Eva heard her and came running out. Reine said she wants her back. Did you know she was out? Because I have to say, I can't believe we never got a courtesy call…"

There was silence on the other end.

"Karen, you there?" He really looked at the phone.

"Yeah, sorry. No, I didn't know she was out. But I'm not her lawyer anymore. I know her father brought in a lawyer of his some time back. What was his name? Gregor Smith, I think. But you're the one who never wanted her in jail, remember? You called me to get involved because of the situation, the circumstances. Even you said you'd have let her walk. Do you need a reminder of everything that went down?"

Of course he didn't, but he didn't know how to explain this awful feeling that he hadn't considered. "I'm not a monster," he said. "Of course I'm glad she's out, but this is about Eva. Remember, the girl Charlotte and I adopted, who is now our daughter? She's not Reine's anymore. So please tell me we don't have anything to worry about."

"You want the truth?"

The knot in his stomach tightened. "No, Karen, I want you to lie to me. What the fuck? Are you telling me there's a chance she could get her back? She signed away her rights. She wanted us to adopt her…"

"Hey, don't yell at me, Marcus. I'm trying to help.

The truth of the matter is yes, she signed away her rights, but in reality, the law isn't black and white. You know this already. In reality, she shouldn't have been in jail, and there are circumstances, although rare, where everything could be reversed. But in this, she would have to prove in court that her decision to sign and relinquish her rights was done under duress or fraud. Remember at the time that the ADA was determined to strip her of her parental rights? She'd lost everything, which is duress. I can only imagine what she was suffering at the time. But, and there is a big but here, you and I both know that in order to accomplish any of this, you'd need a good lawyer, an expensive lawyer. Can she afford this? And that would drag Eva right into the middle of it. Did you try talking to her? She really said she wants her back?"

What was he supposed to say? He'd been shell-shocked, staring at her face through the screen, standing on his doorstep, considering she shouldn't even have known where he lived. How had she found out? He could have handled it better, but surprises were something he'd had more than enough of for one lifetime.

"I probably could have handled it better, but she showed up at the door and wanted to see Eva, and I said no." Actually, he realized he'd said a lot more, and he didn't think he'd ever shake the memory of how her haunted, angry misty blue eyes stared back at him. He knew hatred and anger well.

"You told her no? Why would you do that?"

He could hear her disbelief and wished for a moment that he could go back and re-do the conversation, but he still wasn't sure he'd have let her in the door.

"Karen, I was caught off guard, and it wasn't a friendly visit. She's angry, and maybe she has a right to be, but I don't want that around Eva or my family. And for the record, it was more of a demand, as if she felt she had every right to just show up and see her. You should know that Eva asked her to come to Mom's tonight. But after Charlotte managed to get Eva out of the house and to school, I told her to consider herself uninvited."

Karen hissed. "Marcus, no…"

He could sense she had something more to say, but he continued. "In all fairness, Karen, she shouldn't be there. It's for family, and …"

"And you're not thinking clearly. I get it. But a word of advice, Marcus: Reine is Eva's mother. I always wondered what would happen when she got out, though I didn't expect it to happen this soon. You can't expect her to not play any role in Eva's life. That's not fair. Then there's Eva. She's going to want to know her mother, to see her. You really told her that, Marcus?"

The last thing he wanted was to listen to her reprimands, because he was still reeling from seeing Reine standing there on his doorstep. Marcus didn't like being in any situation where he was caught completely off guard, and he found himself still trying to piece together why she'd gotten out so early, why no one had called him so he could get a plan in place. There was so much he didn't like about this situation.

"She's angry, Karen, and I don't want that around Eva…"

"I hear you, Marcus, but you can't expect her to just disappear. You need to park your anger and what you're feeling and sit down with Reine. And you have to do it for Eva. I love that little girl, and she's a part of our family, but I'm telling you this not as your sister but as a lawyer: Almost every case I deal with is based on anger and resentment because two people won't reasonably sit down and talk and hear each other out. You and Charlotte adopted Eva, so of course you have rights, but so does Reine, and whether you want to hear this or not, big brother, one thing I never doubted was her love for Eva. Her greatest sacrifice was her daughter."

Marcus pushed his door open and stepped out, the phone to his ear now. "That's not what this is about."

"You sure about that? You know I can hear your frustration, and I know you, Marcus. Maybe it's best you don't talk to her. Look, I was planning on coming down this weekend anyway. Do you know how to get a hold of Reine, where she's living?"

Marcus pocketed his keys and gave the door a shove closed. "Just about to find out now. I'm about to pay her parole officer a visit." He looked at the street and the cars going by, the old brick front of the building, as he stepped on the concrete sidewalk.

"You're paying her parole officer a visit? Is it to just find out where she's living and how to get a hold of her, or are you trying to stir up trouble?"

As soon as Karen said it, he stopped at the glass door, which appeared never to have been cleaned. "I'm not an asshole, Karen, but this is my family, my daughter, and I don't want a repeat of the blindside I had this morning. I'm still the sheriff here, and she's on parole, which is very much my business."

"Marcus, tread carefully, because I can still hear the anger in your voice. Another word of advice: You can't be the sheriff on this one, not with Reine. She already has the deck stacked against her."

He took in the door, reached for it, and pulled it open. "I'm not completely heartless. Go back to work. See you when you come up," he said, then hung up before his sister could add one more thing he didn't want to hear.

He tucked his phone in his pocket and made his way down the narrow hall, his footsteps echoing on the cracked old linoleum. He could hear Manny and remembered now how loud he was, and there was that old wood bench. A man was sitting there, tall, lanky, dark skinned, wearing a navy hoodie. He lifted his gaze to Marcus with wariness as he took in the closed door.

"Manny in with someone?" Marcus said, taking in the old door. He lifted his hand and knocked when the man who sat out there said nothing to him.

Then the man only shrugged. "No idea," he said.

Okay, not really helpful, considering even he could hear Manny on the other side. But parolees didn't talk to cops, which was something he was used to.

He tapped on the door, looking down at the man again, who was looking away now, fidgeting.

"Park your damn ass out there and wait your turn!" came the snapped reply.

Marcus figured that was Manny, so he turned the knob and opened the door to look in. Beyond was a short man in a rumpled yellow shirt. Large nose, overweight, with the ruddy complexion of bad health and too much liquor. He was holding a phone, sitting behind an old wooden desk. No one else was in the box of a room. The chair in front of his desk was empty.

"Oh, Sheriff, sorry. Didn't know you were out

there." His voice was gravelly, loud, and the only dark hair he had at the sides and back appeared in bad need of a cut by the messy way it stuck out everywhere. "Hey, listen, I'll call you back. The sheriff just walked in… Yeah, yeah, likely someone on their way back to jail. Sure, six is great. Thanks there, darling."

As he hung up, Marcus took in the windowless office. He thought Manny had packed on a few more pounds, as he struggled to get up with a groan, his thick white chest hair showing from the V of his dress shirt, with its top buttons undone. He shuffled over to the open door as Marcus moved into the room, taking in the two filing cabinets behind the desk, a lateral one and a tall six-drawer one. Both had seen better days.

"You're late, Richie," Manny said to the man waiting. "You just keep your ass parked there until I'm finished with the sheriff."

Marcus took in his desk, the half-eaten burrito with spilled sauce, wrapped in foil, and a supersize takeout cup of a soda. The door was still open, and he could hear the creak of the bench outside.

Manny walked back behind his desk and sat down, then reached for the burrito and took a big bite. It oozed, and sauce dripped onto the desk, so he reached for a napkin from a pile and wiped the sauce from his hand as he chewed. He gestured to the chair opposite him. "So, tell me, which one of my parolees are you here about?" he said without bothering to swallow.

Marcus moved to the door and closed it. There was just something about this man that he'd never liked, his personality, how loud he was, and the feeling he couldn't shake that he wasn't there to help anyone but himself. "Reine Colbert," he said. "She was recently released?"

Manny wiped his face, finished chewing, and swallowed. "Reine? Sure, just a week ago, actually. What did she do? Should have known from that doe-eyed look that she'd be right back in jail."

Marcus rolled his shoulders as Manny dropped his gaze and swiveled around to open the lateral cabinet behind his desk. He pulled out a file and moved his burrito over before opening it and reaching for a pen.

"No, nothing like that," Marcus said. "I need to know where she's living and how to get a hold of her. I assume you know she has a daughter, and the circumstances of her incarceration?"

The man lifted his icy blue eyes to him. Noting the red over his nose and cheeks, his ruddy complexion, Marcus remembered how often he had visited the lighthouse bar. He knew his fondness for cheap draft and cheap whiskey. "Yes, I'm aware of what she was in for," Manny said. "She's a criminal with a record. She signed away her rights to her daughter, and I'm aware you adopted her. So what gives, Sheriff?"

"My wife and I adopted Eva, yes. Reine showed up this morning on my doorstep. I would have expected a courtesy call, yet I heard nothing from the warden of the prison or you, Manny. Would have liked a heads-up, at least."

Manny shook his head. "So she's already violated her parole conditions. Well, there's a surprise." The sarcasm dripped. He slapped her file closed. "She was warned to stay away. I guess you've already picked her up. Great, one more off my plate."

As Marcus stared at the man he didn't like, he could hear his sister's warning, a voice whispering in his ear. "Of course I didn't pick her up," he said. "I'm not a monster. I just would have appreciated a heads-up, is all. I don't like being blindsided. Where is she living, and what's her phone number? She have a job? I want to know all the details, everything."

The man opened the file again and let out a heavy sigh, then reached for a pen and a notepad piled in a messy stack of papers. "She's in a basement suite. Here's the address. No phone number. Got her a job with Better Way Homecare, cleaning. You know, Sheriff, one of her conditions is that she has to stay away from you and her daughter. I'll haul her ass in here and read her the riot act. Better yet, I wasn't planning on doing a home check until Wednesday, but you want me to send a message to her? I don't usually give warnings. I send them back to finish their sentences—and I still might."

He didn't know what to say. He took in Manny, who leaned back heavily in the chair with a squeak, looking at him without feeling. "You want to deliver a message?" he said. "I don't want to know what you're hinting at. I seriously hope the message doesn't involve ransacking her place and scaring her, which I'm sure you've already done. And no, you're not sending her back to jail. That's not why I'm here."

Manny lifted the paper in his grubby thick hands and held it out, and Marcus strode over and reached for it, seeing the address and the reality of what Reine was living through. "You just give me the word, Sheriff, on how you want her handled. If she becomes too much of a problem, I'll see that she gets a refresher on how it works. Nevertheless, if she shows up again, she will be back behind bars, serving her full sentence. I'll make sure she understands how the rules work for her. She's barred from contacting you or her daughter, Sheriff."

Manny scribbled something in what he could only assume was Reine's file.

"Look, I'm not here to have her hassled, and I'm not filing a complaint. I guess I'm more pissed that you didn't pick up the damn phone and call my office to let me know she was out."

Manny leaned back and looked up to him, and something in his expression made Marcus think he never wanted to get on his bad side. "Part of the conditions of her parole is that she's to steer clear of the victims, which includes you and your family. Her daughter is off limits. She knows this, Sheriff. No contact, no nothing. Do you seriously need me to outline how this works? I asked her if her daughter was going to be a problem, and she said no. Don't worry, Sheriff. I know how to handle this. And what I won't tolerate is a parolee lying. As cute as she is, that doesn't give her a pass. I'll see to it she gets a refresher. Now, since you've added to my plate, is there anything else, Sheriff? If not…" Manny lifted his hand and gestured to the door.

Marcus knew it was a dismissal. He shook his head, then lifted the note with Reine's address. "No, but if it's all the same, don't mention this to Reine. I don't want this to be an issue for her or a mark on her record."

The man only stared at him, then pulled in a sharp breath as he looked away, reaching for another file. "I don't tell you how to do your job, Sheriff, so don't come in here and tell me how to do mine. Send Richie in on your way out."

All Marcus could do was step out of the office. He looked down to the man fidgeting with his jeans, which had seen better days. "Your turn," he said.

Then he started walking, shoving the paper in his

pocket, hearing his sister in his head. Now he knew where Reine lived, where she worked. He needed to figure out how to handle the problem of Reine Colbert so that he and his wife and his daughter, Eva, didn't end up with broken hearts.

Chapter Six

R eine was sweaty from the shower when she heard a clatter upstairs, the floor squeaking.

She took in the dingy darkness of the tiny suite she now called home. She could smell the mustiness, the mold. The carpet on the floor had been there decades, if not longer, and the old sofa had springs popping out of it, but the small bed in the tiny bedroom was at least better than the thin mattress she'd slept on behind bars for nearly three years.

She glanced at the small, dated metal insert of a shower as she dried herself off and pulled on a clean pair of underwear, one of her only two pairs. She was already planning how to spend her first paycheck on the few essentials she had to have along with the weekly rent she had to pay for this suite. It was badly furnished, but it was a start to put her life back together.

Then she heard the bang on the door.

"Reine Colbert, open up!"

Her stomach plummeted, because his voice was one she'd never forget.

"Just a minute," she called out, feeling the thud in her chest. She quickly pulled on the same white and blue T-shirt and jeans she'd just stepped out of, then tossed the thin wet towel onto the neatly made bed. She hurried to the door barefoot and flicked the deadbolt, then pulled open the door and took in the fat face and shaggy hair of a man she knew could and would make her life a living hell.

"I didn't know you were coming. I was just…"

He didn't wait for her to ask him in. He pushed past her, bumping her hard and forcing her back. She hoped the people upstairs weren't listening to what was going on. It was humiliating. She was still holding the door, pressed now against the wall, watching the man move through her place, looking around, pulling open a cupboard in the kitchen, a drawer. His dingy dress shirt was tucked into brown tweed slacks.

"This is how it works, sweetheart," he said. "I show up anytime I want. You have any drugs in here, alcohol, guns? You go to work? You been following all the rules?" He didn't look at her as he pulled open her tiny mini fridge, which was empty except for the half sandwich she'd picked up from the reduced section in the grocery store, dated with an expiry of the day before. That had made it cheap, costing only one dollar.

Reine pulled her arms over her chest, knowing her bra was still on the bed, and he was walking into her bedroom, looking around. "I don't have drugs, alcohol, or a gun, and yes, I did go to work. I just got home, in fact."

She could hear him still in her bedroom, pulling open the drawers of the only dresser. She walked the few steps to the bedroom in the cramped suite, seeing her covers now tossed on the floor and the mattress shoved off as if he thought she was hiding something under it. She took in the mess and the way his gaze lingered on her now.

Something was wrong. Her heart hammered as she stood in the doorway, wanting to yell at this jerk, but that would be a mistake.

"You remember all the rules you're to follow?" he said as he stopped right in front of her.

She figured this was what he did, a fat slob who had a few inches on her and at least a hundred and fifty pounds. His breath was warm and foul, and she had to fight the urge to step back.

"Of course I do, and I've stayed out of trouble. I've gone to work and come home."

She was still choked over the fact that Mrs. Hirst's daughter hadn't returned until nearly four, after Reine had run after the old woman when she walked out of the house. By the time she'd made it back to the office, Pete had been gone for the day, so the scrubs were still a wash.

Her parole officer was still standing there with a look in his eyes that absolutely terrified her. Empathy was something she didn't believe he could feel. Maybe it was just an illusion, something she'd once believed existed in people.

"Didn't go anywhere else?" he said, cold, unfeeling.

The knot twisted in her stomach as he let his gaze linger and drag down over her body intimately, all the way to her bare toes. She pressed her hand to her throat, her shirt barely covering her upper chest, feeling the way her heart was hammering. What did he know? This had to be a trick, because she was always looking over her shoulder, something that had stuck with her from being in hell.

"As I said, I went to work. I just got home. Maybe you could do something about the uniform I'm supposed to have for work. My boss hasn't provided it."

He walked into her tiny boxlike bathroom, which was still steamy from the shower, with no ventilation. She knew mold was in and under everything, which was why it smelled so bad. He pulled open the empty cabinet above the sink and made a face, then walked back out, and she took in the mess he'd made, wondering if this was her life now. For how many more years? Five.

"You lying to me about anything there, Reine?" He lifted his hand to touch the edge of her sleeve, running his finger over her arm and up.

She had to fight past the revulsion and look away, reminding herself to breathe in, breathe out. *Just get through this.* "I've stayed out of trouble. Look, what else do you want? I'm just trying to live, to get my life together. I'm a good person."

He dropped his hand and stepped back, then let out a creepy rough laugh. "Let's get something straight here, honey. You're just another convict who's one step from being back in a cage for life. And there's nothing different about you. Once a criminal, always a criminal. You women just find more trouble, and if there's one thing I've learned, it's that every one of you who's sat on the other side of my desk has been the same. You're in for something, and when you get out, you're hooking up with some guy, selling his drugs, stealing and dealing, or you walk into a store and take something, or I find you on a street corner, selling yourself in the sex trade, just another prostitute. Or you're strung out, get yourself fired, and can't hold down another job. I've seen it before. You think you're sneaky with your lying, thinking I don't know what you're doing. But see, I've been doing this for so long that I already know where you're headed, and it took you only four days."

She stared in horror. Could he see her sweating? Her heart was hammering. The way he talked down to her, she wondered whether it was humanly possible to feel even less than she did. "I didn't go to jail for any of that."

"Oh, I know exactly why you went to jail, Reine Colbert," he said sharply. "I have half a mind to revoke your parole, and believe me, I can do that anytime I want with just a snap of my fingers." He lifted his hand and snapped his finger right in her face as if to make a point.

She felt beads of sweat on her forehead. He knew something.

"You forget the rule of staying away from the sheriff, Marcus O'Connell, and the O'Connell family?" he said. "Then there's Eva. You're not allowed to see her. Did you or did you not stop by the sheriff's place and cause a ruckus?"

Her heart thudded. She could see Eva right in front of her, being snatched away. Damn Marcus O'Connell! Why had she thought he wouldn't yank the rug out from under her? He was the same as everyone, cruel.

"I don't know what you heard, but I didn't cause a ruckus, as you call it. I did go to Marcus O'Connell's to let him know I'm fighting for my daughter. I'm going to get her back. I put him on notice…"

"Staying away means you don't visit," he said. "You don't show up at the door. You don't serve anyone with notice. You don't talk to them or walk down the same street as them. There are no warnings in probation. If you screw up and don't follow the rules, there are no second chances. I don't know, Reine. I think your time is up. And don't give me that wide, doe-eyed innocent look. There's nothing innocent about you. You were convicted. Your life is mine, and you're not free to do anything."

"Please, she's my daughter…"

He shook his head. "No, she's not."

Then he pulled his cell phone from his pocket, and all she could see was everything being yanked from her as she stared out from behind bars again. She couldn't do it. She reached out to him as he put his cell phone to his ear. This was it for her.

"Please, no! Don't call. I didn't do anything wrong…"

The moment her hand touched his wrist, his hand flew out, and he backhanded her so hard, hitting the side of her face, her jaw, knocking her head back and to the side. She fell back onto the floor, numb, her head spinning, and then she tasted something metallic, blood…

She realized he was staring down at her, standing over her. Everything in that moment felt surreal as she lifted her hand to her mouth, then pulled it away, seeing blood. His was holding his cell phone and staring at her with the lack of feeling she'd become too used to. She just lay there on the dirty hard floor, knowing she was bleeding, feeling the ache of her jaw, her cheek. As he fisted the hand he'd hit her with, she could see the rage in his face.

"Get up," he said. "Go clean yourself up. You stay

away from the O'Connells and your daughter. You keep your job, you keep your nose clean, and you show up for work and make sure no one takes issue with you for anything. No complaints that you're stirring up trouble anywhere. And you keep your head down and your mouth shut! Do you hear me?"

The way he stood over her, she knew he was untouchable.

She sat up slowly. "I understand," she said, knowing he could do this to her again and again and there was nothing she could do about it. Worse, she knew no one would believe her, and if they did, her only justice would be a one-way ticket back to jail.

"I don't know why you women do this," he said. "It's like you're born this way, too stupid to think, as if you really believe you can lie to me and I won't find out. The next time I show up, it will be with the sheriff's office, and you'll be cuffed and hauled back and shoved in a cage to serve out your full sentence. Could still, because if the sheriff wants to add nuisance charges against you, he'll have that right and you'll serve additional time. Do you understand these rules I've laid out to you?" The way he spoke, she knew the people who lived upstairs would be able to hear everything.

She forced herself to nod, feeling the tightness and ache in her jaw, fighting the urge to lift her hand to her face. "Yes."

He breathed out heavily as he stood over her, and she knew he expected her to stay down. She could feel his anger and what she thought was disgust for her. His nostrils flared as he breathed in and out, pumping his fist, the other still gripping his cell phone. He tucked it into his jacket, gave one last look around, and said,

"Clean up this mess." Then he was at her door, pulling it open. Without looking back, he said, "And if I hear you've been telling stories about me, remember you're just an ex-con. No one will believe you. Me walking out of here now is me giving you a second chance. Don't blow it."

He stepped out and pulled the door closed, and Reine sat there on the floor, fisting her shirt, unable to fight the overwhelming grief that rose up in her. She choked on a sob and cried in silence, realizing Marcus O'Connell was just another man who was kicking her to the curb.

He may have won this round, but next time, she'd be smarter. She was stupid to think she could just walk up to his door.

No, she wouldn't make the same mistake again.

Chapter Seven

Marcus didn't stop at home as he normally would have done before pulling up in front of his mom's place, where he saw Harold's Kia, Tessa's compact, Luke's pickup, and Jenny's Jeep.

"Hey, Marcus."

He took in Brady and his wife, Cassie, holding hands, walking across the grass, both dressed casually in blue jeans. Cassie wore a red cardigan, her dark hair a mass of curls, her dimples poking from her smile.

"You two walk here?"

Brady shrugged. "It's a nice walk, not that far…"

Marcus heard a vehicle and dragged his gaze over to see Ryan pulling in, parking across the road in his park ranger's pickup, and getting out to stride toward him.

"You know what?" Marcus said. "I'm going to have a word with Ryan. See you inside."

He started walking and closed the gap just as he heard the door open behind them. Suzanne's seven-week-old baby boy, Arnie, was crying inside. Then the door closed, and he could hear nothing else.

Ryan stopped in front of him and shook his head. "I was going to call you today, but I've been dealing with a lost hiker. Just finished. Is Reine here?"

Marcus pulled his arms across his chest and turned back to his mom's house, where sheers covered the living room window. It was something they had done for so long so that anyone walking by couldn't see right inside the big picture window. The unease of having the community spotlight on them had never gone away.

"I just got here and haven't been inside, so I don't know," Marcus said. "So how did it go this morning with her?"

Ryan winced as he glanced away. "It didn't," he said, and Marcus could feel that knot in his stomach again.

"What do you mean, it didn't? What the hell is that supposed to mean?"

Ryan gestured toward him. "Look, after you left, I asked her to come over to our place so I could make her some breakfast, have a talk. But she ran out the door. I went to go after her, even called out to her, but she was running up the street. Now, I don't know if it's because she thought I was going to warn her off, but I could see her face, the expression. She was scared. The way you came at her, Marcus, you and Charlotte… But, in all fairness, I don't know what I would do in your place."

"What are you saying, Ryan, that this is my fault? So you didn't talk to her?" He let out a heavy sigh, remembering the address he'd memorized from the paper tucked in his pocket. The place was owned by Wade Wright, a man he didn't know, but he'd spent the afternoon piecing together everything he could about Reine Colbert.

"I never said this was your fault, but I saw a woman

who loves her daughter so much, and the anger between the two of you was like sparks. Maybe I'm seeing both sides, but I'm telling you she wasn't having anything to do with me, not to talk or anything. When she ran off, there was something about her hollow expression. I can't remember having seen that in someone's face before. I feel for her, Marcus. It didn't go well this morning, so a word of advice? Keep your distance from her tonight. Don't say anything here. Just let Eva see her, spend time with her. What would Eva do if she knew you'd tried to keep her mother from seeing her? I saw that little girl this morning and the way she hung on to Reine."

Marcus pulled his hand over his face. He knew his brother was saying this because he cared, but this was his family. "I hear you, but Reine signed away her rights. She asked us to adopt Eva. If she wants to work out something to see Eva now, I'm open to that, but not to her showing up on my doorstep, demanding we give her back. It doesn't work that way, and I won't have that." He lifted his hand, feeling the fury again deep inside, burning. Ryan winced.

"Hey, what are you two doing out here?" Charlotte called out, stepping outside in faded jeans and a yellow T-shirt. Barefoot, she walked across the grass toward him.

"Ryan said Reine ran off and he didn't talk to her. Is she here?" He gestured to the house, not missing the worry still in his wife's face.

"No, she's not, but Eva is inside, telling everyone her mom is coming tonight. Iris pulled me aside and asked me what happened, and so did Luke and Suzanne, so they all know. I've been waiting and worrying because I don't know what to say to her. Do you think we'll get lucky and she won't show?" She stopped beside him and touched his arm, then pressed her hands to her face. "Okay, that sounded awful. I didn't mean it that way."

Marcus wasn't sure what to make of the way Ryan was watching both of them. He slid his hand around her shoulder and turned her, nodding toward the door. Ryan had already started walking.

"I know you didn't, but here we are," he said. "I honestly don't know what to do, but I do know we're going to have to sit down with Reine and talk to her, set some ground rules, something…"

Ryan was inside now, and Charlotte followed behind him, heading to the kitchen. Marcus could hear the voices of his family and spotted Suzanne sitting in the corner of the living room, nursing Arnie. The light was dim, and Jenny was on the sofa, sitting, talking with her, just the two of them alone. He walked down the steps into the living room, hearing voices from the kitchen and from the backyard.

"Heard about your visitor this morning," Suzanne said as she rocked the baby.

Marcus spotted his dad walking toward them, holding two beers, wearing blue jeans and a red and white T-shirt. His dark hair was short and seemed to be lightening more and more every day. Raymond held out a beer to Marcus, who reached for the cold bottle and took a swallow.

"Thanks," he said.

His dad only nodded and kept walking over to the big stool behind him to sit down. Marcus took a step over, feeling his sister and Jenny watching him.

"Owen is barbecuing ribs and chicken," Raymond said. "Will be a while. So is Reine Colbert coming over?

Eva is out back, telling everyone about her mom coming over tonight. She's very excited."

Just hearing the way his dad said it, he felt the twist of the knife in his stomach again. There seemed to be an anvil hanging over his head. He let out a heavy sigh and pulled his hand over his face again.

"I told her not to come," he said, "and Ryan was just filling me in on the talk he didn't have with her."

His dad gave him that pointed look of his, and he knew he was waiting for more. "I was watching out the window and saw the way she ran off," he said. "Ryan called out after her, and when he came over before leaving for work, he said she was spooked and just ran off."

"But not before telling me she wants Eva back," Marcus said. "It doesn't work that way. We're her family now. She can't just take her. And do what with her? She's an ex-con with a record, on probation, living in some shithole—and, what, she thinks I'm just going to be okay with her dragging my daughter to live there? She seems to forget we adopted Eva. She has no rights here. Not anymore."

He knew he needed to get a grip. In the heavy silence, Jenny and Suzanne exchanged a look. He didn't want to hear anyone's perspective, but he knew he was going to get it.

"Marcus, I can hear your frustration," Raymond said, "but you need to dial it back a bit. That little girl out there is so excited about seeing her mother, yet you're already jumping to a fight about keeping her away. I spoke with Karen, and she said she talked to you about the situation. She wanted to come down tonight, but with her being eight months pregnant, Jack has been hovering, and he's insisted on waiting until this weekend. She's worried you might take it too far with Reine. She said something about you paying a visit to her parole officer, maybe finding out where she lives and digging into her life? She's worried you'll stir up trouble for her."

He hadn't expected that from his dad, and he had half a mind to call Karen and tell her to stop sharing everything with him. He knew there was a special bond between the two, and they'd become closer since Raymond had basically returned from the dead.

He shook his head, not missing the matching horror in Suzanne's and Jenny's expressions. "I did pay a visit to Manny, and I have the address where she's living, who she's working for. The rules for her probation include staying away from me, my family, and Eva. She's already violated that…"

"Marcus, no…" Suzanne cut in and winced.

"I told him I don't want it used against her, and that wasn't why I was there. It was just to——"

"To find out everything about her because she has your back to the wall," his dad said, cutting in.

Marcus was beginning to feel how sideways this could go. He glanced over to the front door, wondering when she'd knock and show up. His control was slipping away. He didn't know how to explain to Eva that her mom couldn't just show up there.

"You make me sound horrible," he said. "I'm not unfeeling. Look, Reine should never have gone to jail to begin with, but I couldn't control that outcome then. And, unfortunately, she got dealt a shitty hand. But that's what she has, and she has to live with it. Eva is now our daughter, so there's no way in hell I'm letting any part of this go forward with her thinking she can somehow get her back. She willingly asked us to adopt her…"

His dad gestured to him, and he knew he was getting loud. He glanced behind him to see Ryan walking his way with Luke, whose hair was shorter again, dark and wavy. Those O'Connell blues didn't miss anything, and his white T-shirt showed his bulked-out arms.

"No one is contesting any of that, Marcus, but here's the thing—and maybe I can say this because I had to watch you all grow up from the sidelines, which was the hardest thing I ever had to do. I have an idea of both sides here. That little girl is part of our family, but Reine is still her mother, and that's a bond you can't break. She's going to want a relationship, and the best outcome is working something out so everyone is happy."

His brothers said nothing. Suzanne had finished nursing Arnie and was now burping him, sitting with an overstuffed pillow on her lap.

"I hear you," Marcus said. "Maybe I didn't handle it well this morning. I'll talk to Reine."

Ryan said nothing, and Raymond looked over to Luke. The exchange told him they'd already discussed something.

"Actually, that's something we want to talk to you about," Luke said, cutting in.

"Oh, am I going to want to hear this?" He took in his family in the living room, hearing the tick of the clock and the seconds of silence.

Ryan dragged his hand over his head, ruffling his hair. "You shouldn't talk to her," he said. "I think at this point, Marcus, after this morning, it would be best if we talked to her for you." Maybe Ryan knew he was about to lose it then, as he lifted his hands in the air as if to surrender.

Raymond stood up. "Marcus, you have every right, but think about it. If she's so angry with you and determined to fight you, it would be better if she talked to us. She may just be more willing to listen and be reasoned with. I see your anger, and I understand it, but all you're going to do is butt heads with a woman who's hurting, and that will not make her reasonable, or you. You've got to think about Eva in this. Yes, she's yours, and you adopted her, but that first six years she had with her mom…"

"He's right," Luke said. "And you know it, Marcus. Right now, isn't it about finding a solution everyone can live with?"

Marcus didn't want to agree. He squeezed the cold beer in his hand.

"Marcus, is my mom here yet?" Eva came running in, her long hair in a ponytail. She'd grown from that little girl he'd taken the call for help from. He rested his hand on her head and rubbed it as she reached for his arm, and he could see the joy in her face.

"Not yet," he said. "You know, something could have come up, and…"

"No, Marcus, she wouldn't do that. She said she would come. Is she in trouble or hurt?" She wasn't smiling anymore. From the way everyone was watching him, he knew they were right.

"I'm sure it's nothing like that. She has a job and works. Maybe she had to work longer. How about this? If she doesn't come, I'll go and find her and talk with her…"

"You could pick her up?" Eva was hopeful, staring up at him, and he could see the worry lingering.

"Why don't we just wait a bit? The night's not over yet." He knew the worry she had, and he knew what he'd pulled her from, the nightmares she'd had for so long.

She didn't say anything at first. Then, "You promise?"

He'd never lied to her. He found himself forcing a smile to his lips and running his hand over the top of her head. He gave a tender, teasing yank on her ponytail, which had always brought a smile to her face before. "Go on and have fun with the dog, and let's not jump all the way to worry. If she doesn't come, I'll find her and talk to her. Now go, get your fill of playing with the dog, and tell Owen not to overcook the ribs."

Eva just stood there and looked over to the window with its closed sheers.

Raymond walked over and pulled back the drapes, looking out. "I'll keep an eye out, Eva. Don't worry."

Evidently, that was all she needed to hear, as she walked away. But she turned back in the archway to the kitchen, where he could see Charlotte lingering, chopping something and glancing over to him.

"Marcus, could you make sure Mommy is okay?" she said.

The knot only tightened more in his stomach, because his family was right: He was too close to this. He forced himself to nod. "I will, Eva."

Then she walked away, and his brothers, his dad, Suzanne, and Jenny were all staring at him.

"What?" he snapped.

"Nothing. Just, what's the plan when she doesn't show up tonight?" Ryan said.

Marcus shook his head. "Then I guess you all get your wish and get to talk to her."

He made himself look back over his shoulder to Charlotte, who was watching, listening, and he knew from that one look that this was the thing she'd secretly feared.

Losing Eva.

Chapter Eight

She'd rinsed out the blood from her mouth before looking into the tiny chipped and cracked mirror in the bathroom, taking in her face and loose tooth. Her mouth and jaw were tender from how hard Manny had hit her, and she could see the redness and the slight swelling. She winced when she moved it and knew it was already starting to bruise.

She'd never been hit by a man until she went to prison, where she'd learned the hard way that talking about it and reporting it would only come back on her. She may not have understood before why women who were assaulted didn't report it, didn't get help, but she understood now. The abuser was always heard first, and then came the retaliation, the loss of rights, the cruelty in a world that continued to take everything from her. She had her eyes wide open now.

She took in the mattress and the tossed blankets. Her only clothes had been pulled from the small three-drawer dresser, which was now wide open, onto the dirty old carpet. Well, Manny had made his point. He really could do anything to her. And she knew exactly who had gone to him: Marcus. How had she ever thought there could be a shred of decency in there?

Her legs were shaking as she took in the clock on the stove, seeing it was already seven. Her heart ached with the tears she'd cried over not seeing Eva. This was breaking her. But as much as she wanted to see her, she wouldn't survive if she was sent back to prison.

She reached for the bargain crispy cereal in one of the two old cupboards, grateful at least that Manny hadn't dumped it out to make his point. She opened the box and pulled out the plastic bag in which she'd hidden a cell phone, even though it wasn't logical to hide it. Maybe over time she'd shake all the fears that had come from living behind bars. It had changed her, and she couldn't shake the need to be quiet about everything she had or did.

She unwrapped the black cell phone she'd picked up at a corner store and pulled it out, then dialed, put the phone to her ear, and stared at the closed door, hearing voices outside, likely the people who lived next door or upstairs. Strangers she didn't know, and no one she trusted.

She listened to the ring on the other end, then another as she pulled an arm across her chest,

"Hello?" His voice was deep and low.

"Hi, Dad. It's Reine…"

"Hey, where are you?"

There it was. She had all his attention. She slid her hand to her chest. "That's why I'm calling, to thank you for getting me out, for your lawyer. I'm in Livingston. I have a job, a place… I'm on parole."

Her dad said nothing, and she thought she heard

voices in the background. Where was he, exactly? She didn't know for sure, but it could be the place she knew he had down in Florida with his new wife.

"So you need anything?" he said. "You doing okay?"

She had to remind herself he was her dad, and he cared. How much had he paid for a lawyer to get her out, a good lawyer? More than she would ever be able to repay.

"I'm good, I'm just…" She squeezed the phone, remembering well how her father had cut her out because she'd married a man he didn't want for her. He could be a hard man when people didn't see things his way. "I want to get Eva back." There, she'd said it. "I went to see Eva this morning at Marcus and Charlotte's, and…"

"What are you doing, Reine?" Her dad cut her off quite sharply. "You don't get to have her back. You let those people adopt her. Do you not recall that? I told you not to do it, but you wouldn't listen to me. I told you that you would regret it. I wanted to take her, I told you I would raise her, but do you remember what you said to me?"

There it was, her good old dad, who expected her to fall in line with his way of thinking always. It had been worse after her mother died. The hardness in his voice was a vicious reminder of why it was easier not to talk to him.

"I remember my back was to the wall, and I needed to make sure Eva was okay," she said. "You went to the O'Connells and told me they cared for her, that she was looked after, that they loved her and she was happy. Do you remember that, Dad? You assured me what you saw there was a happy family, and my daughter was okay.

But if you want the truth of the matter, I'll tell you what it felt like, growing up under your thumb. You never listened to me or heard me. I was always to fall in line with your thinking. Remember, do what I say or else? Then there was Vern, my husband, remember? You never showed up for my wedding, your only daughter. And you couldn't bury your dislike of a man whose only sin was not agreeing with you. Vern was his own man, and he wouldn't stay quiet like everyone else when you had an opinion about someone or something that—"

"Oh, here we go. Everything in your life is my fault, and I was a horrible father."

She shut her eyes, because this was going nowhere, the head butting. She could feel herself ready to hang up in anger, but she couldn't do that, because this was about Eva, and she'd swallow anything for her daughter.

"No, Dad, it's not your fault. I never said that. Can we not fight, please? Eva being with the O'Connells was the best thing for her, and unfortunately, being locked up, I didn't have the luxury of imagining what if. But I'm out now, and she's my daughter, Dad. I want her back. I'm her mother…"

She heard the deep sigh on the other end before she'd finished.

"Reine, you gave her away. You signed away your rights and let them adopt her. I told you that once you did that, she wouldn't be yours anymore. I did everything to reason with you, telling you not to go that far…"

"I had no choice. I had to do what was best for Eva, and at the time, seeing she had stability with people who loved her and wouldn't let anything happen to her was what I needed for her. If they adopted her, no one from social services could walk in and shove her somewhere else where she wouldn't be okay. I listened enough to the stories of other mothers locked up, their kids separated and pulled away from them for no reason but that some bureaucrat decided so. Those kids were always tossed in some place that was worse than before. I couldn't have that. Marcus and Charlotte, I knew they cared for her and would protect her and keep her safe, but I'm her mother, and now I'm out, and as much as they say they care for her and love her, I'm still her mother…"

"And what can you provide her, exactly? A home? Stability? Isn't that what landed you in the mess you were in? You may be her mother, Reine, but you think you can walk back in and just take her? She's not yours anymore. I don't know how to get you to understand. Sometimes things can't be fixed…"

"Well, there is a way, and a good lawyer can present that argument. One good thing about being in prison is that you hear things, and I heard someone say something her lawyer had told her about the kids she'd given up in jail. There are circumstances where an adoption can be overturned, like in cases of duress or fraud. The DA tried to strip me of my parental rights. Wouldn't that fall under both?"

She had all the arguments running through her mind already—the poverty she'd been forced into after losing everything, the nightmare of living on the streets and meeting Tommy. Not a day went past that she hadn't thought of the man who'd been the only one to offer a helping hand, as flawed and screwed up as he was. She still relived the horror of that night over and over, playing through the what-ifs in her mind. What if she hadn't gone along with him? What if she hadn't handcuffed Marcus?

"Reine, you always had unrealistic expectations. What you're talking about is years of legal fighting, and lawyers cost money. I got you out, but Gregor Smith wasn't cheap. I had to put the cottage in Maine up for sale to pay his bill, and Lori wasn't happy about that."

She knew his second wife was two years younger than she was. She'd never met her and realized she didn't want to.

"I'm sorry you had to sell your second home," she said. Or was it his third? She wasn't sure anymore what he had. "But I appreciate what you did for me, putting the money out. I'll pay you back. I don't know how, but I'll do it." She fisted her hand, realizing she'd have to swallow it, but for Eva, she'd get down on her knees and beg.

"Oh, stop it. You couldn't even put a roof over your head before. How the hell are you going to pay me back? You're my daughter, Reine." There it was, another slap before he went back to his fatherly duty.

"Dad, we lost everything when my husband had cancer. His health insurance with the fire department started denying coverage, finding loopholes. I was stuck with hundreds of thousands in medical bills. They took our house, and my wages were garnished. You make it sound as if it was my fault…" The minute she said it, she realized he'd never understand, and he didn't like being painted into a corner, having anyone point out to him that he could be wrong. "Look, I didn't call you to fight or argue, Dad. I need help…please."

He said nothing. It was always that silence with him that got her. "I'd do anything for you, Reine. You're my daughter. But I gave you a choice before, and if you had listened to me, we wouldn't even be having this conversation and I wouldn't be tossing away all this money."

She could hear the no coming. She pressed her thumb and forefinger to the bridge of her nose and looked down, shutting her eyes tight, feeling a tear slip out. "Please, Dad, do you want me to beg?" Her voice caught, and she willed herself to pull it together. Her dad wasn't a man who dealt with emotional women. He expected her to pull it together. That was how he'd raised a teenage daughter eating her heart with grief. Her mother had been the glue that held them together. "Sorry, I'm just really tired. But I'll do anything. Please…" She kept her voice even, calm. She had to with him.

"I'll talk to Lori about it, but hear me on this, Reine. You'll need to listen to me this time if I do this."

She nodded. She knew that would mean him telling her what to do, what he expected, but right now she'd agree to anything. "And Gregor Smith, you'll call him?"

"Reine, I'll talk to Lori first, because this affects her too. Gregor Smith isn't cheap. If we do this, you have to do everything he says, everything we say. That's the only way this works."

There was something about his terms that she'd never been able to live with, but when she had nothing, she knew there was no other way.

"I understand, Dad. Thank you."

He mumbled a rough goodbye, and she held her cell phone, pressing it to her forehead.

Hearing a knock on her door, she grabbed the plastic bag, her heart hammering, wondering whether Manny was back. She shoved the cell phone inside it and back into the cereal box deep enough that the crispy rice covered it.

"Just a minute," she called out, putting it back in the cupboard and closing it before walking barefoot to the solid old door, wishing she at least had a peephole to look through, that early warning so she knew who was on the other side.

She closed her eyes for a second, her heart hammering, and then turned the knob and pulled the door open. Staring back at her was Ryan O'Connell with a woman and two men she'd never seen before, and Marcus was in back behind all of them.

Her heart sank, and she squeezed the knob, feeling that anger and fear coming from nowhere. All she said was, "What do you want?"

Was he there to arrest her? Maybe Manny was being true to his word.

She'd expected Marcus to grind her into the ground, but he said nothing. Instead it was Ryan who stared at her with an odd look and said, "We came to have a talk, Reine. Can we come in?"

There it was, the one thing she did have control over. She kept her hand on the door.

"I don't think that's a good idea," she said. "In fact, just you being here, all of you..." She dragged her gaze, taking in each of them, wondering who they all were. "You're putting a target on me and could have me back behind bars. Unless that's why you're here."

"No, Reine, that's not why we're here," Marcus cut in from in back. He was tall, all the men were, and she had to look up. Even the woman with long hair pulled back in a ponytail was taller than she was. "But I want to know first, who did that to you?"

There was something about him when he spoke. She realized she wanted to believe he cared, but she couldn't do that, not ever again. She made herself look away from him, her hand on the door, wondering, if she could just close it, would they walk away and leave her be?

Reine kept her mouth shut and forced herself to give her head a shake, taking them all in. Were they all family, the ones she didn't know? "Nothing happened. Now, I'm going to say it only once more. Please leave."

This time she went to close the door, but a hand reached out and slapped it, Ryan. The sound shot right through her, and she jumped back, feeling the fear again, her hand going to her chest, her heart hammering, stepping back again and again. When he stepped inside, she struggled to catch her breath, her back against the wall.

A hand reached out and touched her shoulder, and she took in the woman, who said, "Someone hurt you. Reine, I can see you're terrified."

Her breath caught as she stared at this woman she didn't know. "Who are you?" was all she got out.

Her eyes were a vivid blue, looking down at her. "I'm Suzanne O'Connell, and we're not leaving until you tell us who did this to you."

Chapter Nine

Marcus took in the basement suite in a house he knew was at least a hundred years old. He could smell the mustiness in the dingy tiny place, and he glanced at the papers, a sweater on the floor, a small table knocked over. From the open door to the bedroom, he spotted a mattress pulled off the bed, blankets and clothes tossed. Suzanne was standing in front of Reine.

He knew when someone was terrified, and from what he was seeing, something bad had happened. He also knew when someone had been hit. Her face, her jaw… He'd been in enough scrapes on the wrong side of the law and had been hit more times than he could remember, so he knew what a punched face looked like.

Then there was fear, something else he'd seen too many times.

Owen was in the doorway of the bedroom, and Marcus watched his dad in the kitchenette, looking at the little there was. Ryan was standing off to the side.

The outside door was still open to where Jenny's Jeep, which they'd all squeezed into, was parked behind an older-model blue Cavalier with its side mirror missing, a rusty old pickup, and what looked like ten old garbage cans filled with junk.

He could hear the compassion in Suzanne's voice as she again said, "Come on, tell me who did this to you."

Reine had said nothing ever since Ryan slapped the door open, but he'd seen the fear, the catatonia. The picture he was seeing there was something else he'd seen far too often.

"Marcus…" Owen said from the bedroom of the tiny suite.

Marcus was chewing a piece of gum as he walked around his dad, who was now just standing, watching, saying nothing, and Ryan, who was shaking his head. He didn't have to say anything to his brothers or his dad. They had to see what he was seeing.

"You think this has anything to do with her face?" Owen said in a low voice as Marcus stepped into the boxlike room, where the single mattress had been tossed over, the blankets and clothes strewn, and the drawers pulled open. He took two steps to the bathroom and flicked on the light, seeing old and dingy.

"Looks like someone was angry. A break-in, maybe? Someone hit her," Marcus said.

From the way his brother was looking at him, he wondered whether he expected him to do something. "So is this an active crime scene, or do we clean it up?" Owen said.

Marcus didn't know how to reply. He let out a heavy sigh and stepped back out into the cramped main living space, seeing the old tweed sofa, the tiny side table knocked over, no kitchen table or chairs, a mini fridge, and an old rusty stove. He had to wonder whether it worked.

"Reine, who did this to your place? Was there a break-in? Who hit you?" he said.

Suzanne stepped back to reveal Reine, whose big eyes were still spooked.

Reine shook her head. "You mean you don't know?" she said so sharply, so accusingly, that it had everyone looking at him.

"I wouldn't be asking if I knew," he said. "Look, just tell me who it was and I'll go and pick him up, hold him accountable, and make sure he leaves you alone."

The fear was gone from her expression, and the anger was back. She glanced once to his sister, who he realized was a voice of reason. Reine shoved her fingers in her hair, dragging it away from her face, unwilling to share anything. Her lip was starting to swell.

"I highly doubt that," she finally said, "considering this was a warning because of my visit to you this morning. You mean you aren't responsible for this?" There it was, the accusation again. "You think I want this getting back to Manny? You already told him I was at your place, and now here you are. Is this your way of seeing that I'm tossed back behind bars and will never be able to see my daughter? I guess that's one way for you to solve a problem, isn't it?"

He heard a hiss and thought it was Suzanne.

"Who's Manny?" Ryan asked, dragging his gaze over to him. Owen was standing beside him. He realized now that Manny had taken his visit that morning as an excuse to really bring the hammer down on Reine.

"Manny Meskill, Reine's parole officer," he said in a

low voice, looking around, then dragged his gaze back to Reine. "Did he hit you?"

She pulled her arms over her chest. The look she gave him was hard, that of a woman who had shut down. When had she decided to hate him? It was clear she wasn't about to offer anything.

"Can he do this?" Owen said to him.

He wanted to say no, but the truth was that he could do anything to his parolees and would always be given the benefit of the doubt. "Unfortunately, he just has to say he had reasonable cause, and the way the laws work, he's believed over a convicted felon. His story just has to be better." He pulled his hand over his face, looking over to Eva's mother, knowing it would upset his little girl to see her mom like this. He wanted to kick Manny's ass. "I'm sorry, Reine," he said. "I went to see Manny to find out where you lived. I didn't do it to stir up trouble for you."

Her arms were still crossed, pulled tight across her chest. She angled her head, disbelief in her expression, her eyes. She wasn't about to be reasonable. Anger was anger. "Now, why don't I believe that?" Sarcasm dripped from her tone. "This morning, you warned me off. Then, after my daughter was so happy to see me and asked me to come to your mother's place, you told me clearly that I wasn't welcome. Isn't that what you said? So forgive me if I don't believe you, Marcus O'Connell. I'm very clear on how this works, being warned off from my seeing my daughter, from contacting her, you, or your family. You know these ridiculous rules make no sense. Any contact like this is a one-way ticket back to prison for me. I'll serve out my entire sentence, with additional time tacked on for whatever you decide to charge me with." She gestured sharply.

He felt everyone watching him. "Reine, I wouldn't do that. Yes, the truth of the matter is that when you showed up on my doorstep this morning, I was thrown. You never told me you were getting out. If you'd only called first, talked to me, we could have worked something else out. But we adopted Eva. You know this, you wanted it to happen, and now you suddenly show up to have her back? What is the plan here, Reine? Are you gong to hire a lawyer and try to reverse the adoption? I spoke with Karen already…"

Her jaw slackened, the hurt back in her expression. He felt a hand on his shoulder, Owen, his big brother, as if he needed a reminder that he shouldn't be there. He glanced back to him.

Owen shook his head and said, "Not helping, Marcus. Give me a hand in here." He nodded to the bedroom, where Ryan was already standing, looking at the mess.

Reine hurried around Suzanne to where they crowded into her bedroom. "What are you doing? Am I not entitled to any privacy?" she yelled at Ryan, who had reached for the mattress, Owen grabbing the other end.

This was not a woman who could be reasoned with. Marcus knew when emotions could turn a situation volatile.

"Reine, you're upset," Owen said in that calm way he had. "We're just helping to clean up, make this right."

Marcus watched them put the mattress back on the bed.

Reine reached down and grabbed the blankets before they could. "You want to make this right? Then leave, now," she said sharply.

How was he going to get through to her that he wasn't trying to make her life difficult? He felt another tap on his shoulder and took in his dad, who gestured to the doorway, where he realized there was no door. He followed him out to the small kitchenette.

"I understand you want to handle this and wouldn't stay behind and let us talk to her," Raymond said. "But she's right. She's in a bad spot here, and this authoritative abuse is a result of your actions. I'm not saying it's your fault, but she's not going to hear reason if you're here. I can already see her digging in and coming at you. She's angry and hurt. I can see from her face, the fear, that she sees you as a threat. I know what her parole officer did, putting the fear of God into her.

"He really did a number, likely threatened her with everything that could happen, revoking her parole, tossing her back behind bars. He made a mess of her place, looking for something. You know how this works. If he's pissed enough, something will be planted, and she won't be believed because she's a criminal. She'll never get any justice for what he did to her face. If she came clean and told you, could you actually arrest or charge her parole officer? You and I both know what a man can do to a woman. She's not going to say a word to you, and if she did, in how many different ways would it come back on her?"

It was the way his dad spoke that bothered him more than anything, because he didn't want to admit he was right.

"Meskill can't go around hitting people." Marcus

pulled his arms across his chest, watching as his sister opened the fridge and looked inside, then pulled open a cupboard, which held a box of cereal and nothing else.

He walked over to the doorway, where he could hear the back and forth. He thought his brothers were trying to calm Reine, who, he could hear from the pitch of her voice, had gone right back to not being reasoned with.

"The DA would never prosecute," Marcus said. "And Reine's right that she'd likely find herself back in prison. Meskill's story could be anything, that it wasn't him, that she did it herself, or that she came at him, which is assault on her part. Whatever she claims, a judge would toss it right out. In fact, I'd be ordered to charge Reine with something else, and I wouldn't have a choice. I can't believe this. I'm not a monster. I'm not looking to jam her up. I just want…"

"I know, but, Marcus, you have to hear us. Listen to what Ryan and Owen said, and Suzanne. After seeing her reaction to you, I can tell there's no way you can reason with her. She's angry with you. She's not going to be reasonable with you because she blames you for this, and maybe for everything. What's the outcome here, Marcus? You want her completely out of Eva's life? Because I've got to tell you, she's her mother. Take it from someone who was forced from his own kids' lives and had to watch from a distance, although for different reasons completely. I understand where she's coming from, and you too."

"What are you saying, that I have to give up Eva? I'm not doing that. We adopted her, Charlotte and I. We're her parents now…"

"No, I'm her mother," Reine said.

Marcus turned to the woman staring daggers at him.

He hadn't realized she'd heard him. His dad touched his arm.

"Reine, that's not what Marcus means," Owen said, walking around her and Ryan, who was still lingering in the doorway. "We all know you're Eva's mother, and nothing can change that. But Marcus is right that he and Charlotte adopted her and are now her parents, her legal guardians. You can't expect to just walk back in and be a parent to Eva, not when you're living in a place like this. Do you have a job? What will happen to Eva? Will she hang out here, or what? What's the plan?"

Reine shook her head, pulling into herself, shutting down. "I know what's best for my daughter," she said. "You're right that I asked you to adopt her, and I'd probably do it again so Eva would be safe and protected, but let me be clear, Marcus O'Connell. I've had a lot of time to think and put things in perspective."

From the way she spoke, he could see the burning hatred. He said nothing, watching her pull her arms over her chest, seeing how thin she was.

She glanced away as if she wasn't supposed to look at him, then pulled in a sharp breath. "I wish I'd never met you, Marcus. Now please leave," she said, her voice catching.

He felt a hand on him again and knew he could fix nothing here.

"Come on," Owen said.

His dad had already walked to the door and pulled it open, and one by one, his brothers walked out, followed by Suzanne and his dad. Marcus stopped in the doorway and turned back to this woman who'd had the shit kicked out of her, wondering how to explain to her that if it hadn't been for him, she'd likely have been facing life in prison rather than making it out in a few years as she had.

But he knew the woman he was looking at now could see none of that.

"I'm sorry, Reine," he said. "I really am."

Chapter Ten

R eine ate the rest of the half sandwich, tasting the off-ness of the deli meat, but at least she wouldn't be hungry. She downed a glass of water before shoving on her shoes, seeing the hole in the toe and picturing her first check, which she expected next Thursday. She'd pick up groceries first, just the items she knew would be on sale, and maybe a new pair of shoes.

When she heard a knock on the door, she stared at it and instantly went to her feet. The alarm that shot through her was an unwelcome friend that had been there too long. There was just something about visitors, first Manny and then the O'Connells. She feared the next would be a cop there to arrest her and drag her back to jail. Maybe Marcus himself. Something whispered in her ear that reality was just around the corner.

She had to swallow the panic that was choking her and had her struggling to pull in a breath. Her legs shook as she stood, but she made herself take a step to the door, her heart hammering again, her hand fisted and damp as she rested it on the doorknob and squeezed. She pressed her forehead to the door and shut her eyes for a second, pleading for nothing bad to be there.

Then she pulled it open and blinked as she took in Suzanne O'Connell, a smile on her face and a paper bag of groceries in her arms.

Like, what the hell was this?

"Good morning," Suzanne said. "I hope you slept okay. Listen, I felt so bad over what happened last night. It could have been handled better than it was. Now, I'm probably completely overstepping. Apparently it's one of my many flaws, as has been pointed out by my brothers and my husband. But I took a chance you would still be here, and I brought you groceries. Can I come in?"

Reine wasn't sure what expression was on her face as she gripped the door. The sandwich was sitting like lead in her stomach. Suzanne was still standing there, not pushing her way in—yet. She was bringing her groceries?

"I don't understand," she said, looking past her.

Maybe Suzanne understood, as she shook her head and said, "It's just me. Marcus isn't here, or the rest of my family. In fact, they don't know I'm here. Well, just Harold, my husband, because he's looking after the baby before he has to go to work." She was rambling in this over-the-top happy way.

Reine stepped back and motioned inside. "Why not?"

Apparently, that was all Suzanne needed, as she strode in with a bright smile and set the paper bag on the chipped and marked-up kitchen counter. Reine looked out, seeing a light blue Kia parked behind the pickup and three other cars beside the mess of garbage cans.

She closed the door and watched as Suzanne, a stranger, put eggs, milk, and cheese into her fridge. Reine walked over, seeing dish soap, a new sponge, bread, butter, peanut butter, and chicken, as well, along with two of cans of what she thought was soup. She just stared and couldn't make sense of what this was.

"I don't understand why you're doing this," was all she could get out as she watched this woman invade her space and fill her fridge. Her mouth watered as she took in the sandwich meat, lettuce—and was that really a small jar of mayonnaise?

Suzanne was tall, with long hair hiked back in a ponytail, in blue jeans and a bulky T-shirt. She closed up Reine's tiny fridge, which was now full. "You had no food, Reine. I saw that last night when we were here. And I didn't know what to do, seeing how upset you were after what happened to you." She turned and gestured to her face as if she needed a reminder of the smackdown she'd taken.

Her hand went up and touched the tender side of her face as she took in Suzanne, who had the same eye color as her brother. The resemblance was there. She still didn't know what this was.

"I took a minute last night, trying to figure out what I'd do if I were in your spot," Suzanne said.

Reine just stared at this woman, Marcus's sister, who was folding up the paper bag as if she needed something to do, looking over to her. All Reine could see now was the box of granola bars and cookies on the counter.

Reine realized Suzanne had stopped talking and was now watching her with her lips pressed tight and an odd, sad smile. Reine couldn't get her tongue to move.

"It may not be much," Suzanne said, "but I figured, seeing that you had some food in your cupboards, your fridge was a start. You're just out of jail, just working?"

Reine knew it was a question, and she forced herself to nod, not missing the way Suzanne's gaze lingered on the side of her face and her jaw, where the swelling had left a nice green and blue hue.

Suzanne reached into her pocket and pulled out a tube of what looked like concealer, which she held out to her.

"What is this?" Reine said.

"Your face, the bruising. Anyone looking at it will know you've been hit. This will hide some of the bruising, at least, so you don't have people asking questions you can't answer."

She stared at the small tube of concealer and then the door. "I have to go to work. Thanks for this and the food… I just don't understand why you're doing this, why you're being so nice."

Maybe this was Suzanne's way of getting Reine to walk away from her daughter. Her distrust burned.

Suzanne lifted both her hands in surrender and shook her head. "I have no ulterior motive, I assure you. You're Eva's mother, and I know what happened to you, what you went through. You have to know we never believed you got a fair shake, none of us. What happened to your husband? He was a firefighter?"

Reine wondered when the floor would collapse beneath her, leaving her shellshocked and down again.

She didn't welcome anyone bringing up her dead husband, Vern.

"Well, I used to be a firefighter here, once upon a time," Suzanne said, "until I was forced out, which is another story. But I know what happened to your husband wasn't right or fair, and it has happened to too many firefighters in this country. Medical insurers look for any way to pull funding and any loophole to get out of paying, citing clauses about pre-existing conditions. Suddenly, that first responder's family has nothing, loses everything because medical bills are not covered. You were screwed, Reine, you and Eva and your husband, and I'm sorry for that.

"When I left last night, I racked my brain trying to figure out what I could do to help you, and one of the things you learn first in an emergency is triage. So here is triage, food so you can eat. I want to take that one worry off your plate. It's a start, Reine. I'm not the enemy. It's just that if I were in your position, I would want someone to give a damn and give me a helping hand. I can see you think there's something more, but I assure you there isn't. It's just food. It doesn't come with strings."

She wasn't sure she believed her, even though she wanted to. That was a trap she wouldn't let herself fall into.

"Well, thank you…" she said before glancing at the small old digital clock. The time was eight sixteen, and panic shot through her as she thought of how long it would take her to get to work. This time, if she was late, her job would be gone. "Oh, shoot, I've got to go. I'm late, and I can't be late…"

"I'll drive you. Go put that on your face," Suzanne said with a sympathy she didn't understand.

Reine hesitated only a second before hurrying to her bathroom with the tube of concealer and flicking on her light, hearing rustling from her kitchen. She took in the swelling she couldn't hide, and she squeezed the cover-up on her fingers and gently smoothed it over the bruising, careful with the tender spot, which still hurt.

What did Suzanne O'Connell really want? There had to be something.

She took in her face, seeing it had helped some. At least the blue and green bruise wouldn't be the first thing people saw. She rinsed her hands and took in her faded blue and white T-shirt, her old grey hoodie, and the same blue jeans she'd worn the day before. She knew there was nothing she could do about her clothes.

She dried her hands on the thin old towel, flicked off the light, and strode out, seeing Suzanne at the door, pulling it open and nodding to her.

"Can barely see it from here," she said. "Let's go."

She followed Suzanne out the door and pulled it closed before shoving her only key in the lock and turning it. She tucked it into her pocket and took one step, and Suzanne handed her a granola bar.

"Here," she said. "Not sure if you've eaten yet, but at least you've got it."

She took in the green wrapper and tucked it into her pocket as well as she hurried to Suzanne's car, where she pulled open the passenger door and slid onto the cloth seat. She pulled the door closed and reached for the seatbelt as Suzanne put the car in reverse and backed out.

"I'm sorry if I seem a little defensive," Reine said.

"It's right at the end of this block. Take it all the way down to Graham Street…"

"Better Way Homecare?"

Reine found herself staring at the woman, suddenly feeling the rug being yanked out from under her again. How the hell did she know that?

Suzanne must have known she was right when Reine didn't answer, as she drove fast down the street and glanced once her way. "Marcus told us last night. He found out where you lived and worked. That's just something about our family. We tend to share everything. Don't freak out about it."

She said nothing at first, wondering why it seemed she had a target on her. "Well, I guess that shouldn't surprise me. So should I expect a visit at work from the sheriff? Maybe my boss will get a visit, too, and next I'll be out of a job. Or is this where I hear the warning that if I want to keep my job, have a roof over my head, and stay out of jail, I need to walk away from my daughter? Because if that's the case, you can pull over right now and let me out, and I'll say thank you for the food, but stay the hell away from me."

Suzanne wasn't smiling. She just shook her head.

Reine's go-to was anger. She couldn't shake the fury that seemed to be her constant companion and had her wanting to yell and scream and rage at the world.

"You have it all wrong, Reine," Suzanne said. "That's not what this is about. And Marcus wouldn't do that. I can see you already have your mind made up, but my brother isn't the bad guy here. None of us are. He told us he didn't handle it well when you showed up yesterday at the door, when you said you wanted Eva back. It scared my brother and Charlotte. You have to know we love that little girl. She's part of our family, Reine. Even though I want a peaceful resolution here, my showing up this morning with groceries and driving you to work is just that. Don't make me the bad guy, too, because I'm not. In fact, Marcus doesn't know I'm here. You have to know how upset Eva was last night when you didn't show up. She told all of us, and I've never seen her so excited, so scared, so nervous. Then there was the way she cried when you didn't show."

Hearing Suzanne talk about her daughter and how upset she had been only added to the giant hole in her heart, which she didn't think would ever heal. Suzanne turned left and gave the car gas, driving toward the front of the concrete strip mall. She took in the sign for Better Way Homecare and could see Ivy just getting out of her car.

"So she thinks I deserted her again," Reine said. "I bet Marcus loved that."

The ache that seemed to be her familiar companion had her wincing and her eyes burning. This wasn't the time to fall apart. Everything she did was for her daughter, breathing, living. Suzanne pulled into the lot and parked in front of the glass industrial door just as Ivy pulled it open and glanced back to her in the car. She took in the clock in the car, seeing she was early by ten minutes. At least she hadn't screwed this up. She felt a hand reach over and touch her arm.

"Reine, please, whatever you think of my brother, he's not a monster," Suzanne said. "He told her it wasn't your fault, that some grownup stuff happened, but he promised her he would check on you, make sure you were okay, and that she would see you. Marcus is not going to let Eva think the worst of you, as if she could.

Don't jump to automatically accusing Marcus of driving a wedge between you. He feels bad over what your parole officer did to you. We all do. But he's reasonable. Please, Reine, all I ask is that you find a way to be reasonable, too."

Reine reached for the door, feeling Suzanne's hand still on her arm. She let her gaze slip to it until Suzanne pulled her hand away, and Reine gave the door a hard yank open and stepped out before looking back to Marcus's sister, still unable to figure out what this was.

"Thanks for the ride," she said.

Suzanne only nodded.

Reine closed the door just as Ivy stepped back out from the office in pink scrubs with the Better Way logo on front, carrying a tote, her gaze lingering on Reine's worn jeans.

"Pete wasn't here when I finished yesterday, so I can't do anything about what I'm wearing," Reine said.

Ivy propped open the glass industrial door with her foot and nodded to Suzanne's car, which was just backing out. "See you got a ride, a nice car. Who is that?"

The last thing she wanted to do was share anything personal with Ivy, especially the O'Connell name. Paranoid or not, she knew it would find its way back to her parole officer.

"A friend, is all," she said "Is Pete in? I'll ask him now about the uniform." She went to step inside.

Ivy wasn't smiling, not moving from where she stood in the open door. "Yeah, he's in his office, waiting for you. Not sure what you did, Reine, but I can't remember Pete ever being so angry. He's in a mood this morning." Then she let go of the door and walked to her car.

Reine took in the closing door and froze, terrified of what was waiting for her on the other side. She listened to the slam of the car door behind her, feeling the constant cycle of terror, and for the first time in her life, she wondered if running was now her only choice.

Chapter Eleven

Marcus was sitting on the edge of his desk when Charlotte walked into his office.

"What do you want to do about Eva?" she said. "She was asking about Reine again this morning when I dropped her off at school. She asked if she could call her mom, where her mom was living, and if she could go there and see her. I don't know what to tell her, Marcus. I see that desperation in her eyes. I haven't seen her so unsettled in a long time. Damn Reine for coming back and doing this to Eva!"

He was staring at the file Harold had given him, the image of the man he suspected was starting the fires. He handed the mug shot and file back to Harold, knowing his deputy would handle it while Charlotte was venting.

"You bringing him in?" was all he said to Harold, who dragged his gaze from him to Charlotte and then back. Maybe he expected him to answer Charlotte about Reine, but that was exactly what Marcus didn't want to talk about.

"I'll handle it," Harold said. "I'll head out to his

place, have a word with him, see what I can spot lying around in the open. But I think I'll just keep an eye on him, watch him the next few nights. I already know whatever he's doing, he's doing it under the cover of darkness. I have no solid proof that will stick yet, just my gut, which isn't enough for anything. Catching him in the act would be like a gift."

Marcus only nodded, then pulled in a breath. He didn't know what to do to ease the sorrow that had nearly killed him the night before when he'd carried a crying Eva to Charlotte's car. He knew she'd cried herself to sleep.

Maybe Harold was waiting for him to say something else, but Charlotte lingered in the doorway, her arms crossed, and he could see how tense she was. She was the mother of his children, who wouldn't let anything happen to them.

"Charlotte, I don't know what to do about Reine," he finally said. "Ideally, we'll come up with some solution to stay in touch, have her over to see Eva every now and then. I guess it's wishful thinking that she'll stay out of her life. But Reine is angry at me, at us. I don't know…" He lifted his hands. When dealing with someone he couldn't reason with, he knew the best solution was to walk away. But he couldn't walk away from this, because it involved Reine and Eva.

Harold was still standing there, and baby Arnie, who had been sound asleep in his carrier, started fussing from the small table by the window behind him.

"So where did you say my sister was?" Marcus said.

Harold scooped his son from the carrier and patted his bottom. "Yeah, you're wet, aren't you?" he said to the baby before looking over to him. His gaze lingered a second, hesitating. Marcus could see that Harold didn't quite know what to expect from Suzanne at times.

"She went to the grocery store as soon as it opened," he said.

Marcus shrugged and looked back over to Charlotte, still trying to figure out the Reine situation.

"To buy groceries for Reine," Harold continued.

Marcus dragged his gaze back to him.

"Hey, look, she was upset," Harold said. "I don't think she slept more than a few hours last night, and she was out of bed before I was, out the door, telling me to watch Arnie. She sent me a text as I was leaving the house that she'd pick him up at the station. This is your sister we're talking about. You know that once Suzanne makes her mind up about something…"

Marcus let his jaw slacken, remembering when his dad had said the night before that Reine's cupboards were empty except for a box of cereal. He shut his eyes. Maybe he should have been the one to go. He realized Charlotte didn't know, because last night had been all about a crying Eva.

"Well, that's good," Marcus said. "Shit, you know, I should have done that." He shrugged again, taking in the way Charlotte was looking at him, and gestured toward her. "She had next to nothing there, like nothing. Then there's Manny. Haven't figured out yet what to do about him. What he did to Reine… I know you need to keep eyes on this arson case, Harold, but I also want you to dig around on Manny Meskill. He assaulted Reine, her face. He shouldn't have done that, and it's only making this situation worse. When Therese comes in, maybe have her look through his background, see what skeletons you can dig up."

Harold only nodded and walked to the door, and Charlotte moved aside, running her hand over a fussing Arnie, who was kicking his legs and waving his little fists in the air.

"You want me to change him for you?" she asked, holding her arms out.

Harold stepped around her and shook his head. "No, I got him. As soon as Suzanne shows up, I'll start digging, but what do you want me to look for?"

Marcus pulled his arms over his chest. "Any red flags. Reine's face, he hit her hard. A man who does that has done it before. See if any complaints have been filed about him. Look into his personal life, relationships…"

"And what about Reine? Can you get her to file a complaint?" Harold said.

Marcus took in Charlotte. He could see the confliction there. He turned back to Harold, hearing the baby really fussing now. "No, she can't." He let out a sigh and then stood up.

Harold let his gaze linger on him and then Charlotte before giving his head a shake as he stepped out. Marcus wasn't sure he agreed.

Charlotte strode toward him, and he could see how unsettling this was for her. "So he gets away with hitting a woman?" she said.

"He gets away with hitting an ex-con on parole. She doesn't have rights, and the deck is stacked against her. If she files a complaint against her parole officer, she won't be believed, even with bruising on her face. It's the way the system is set up. You know anything about slavery laws?"

Charlotte frowned.

"Most people think slavery happened way back

when, and it was abolished, but what they don't under-stand is how the system works, really works. Yeah, the Thirteenth Amendment abolished slavery at the end of the Civil War—that is, until you commit a crime and are convicted. Then…" He took in the shock in Charlotte's expression, and he could see she understood his deeper meaning. "So now, because of old laws that shouldn't still be on the books, she's suffering the consequences. She has difficulty finding a job or housing and loses access to the rights and government benefits you and I have. Then there's the right to vote. Not every state has changed its laws yet.

"That punishment clause is still there, and it was never more apparent to me than when I saw Reine last night. And don't forget, too, she can't just walk around freely like you and me with no consequences. Because she showed up on our doorstep the way she did, she's already violated the rules of her parole, which means a one-way ticket back to prison. The DA won't charge Manny, because Reine has no rights in the eyes of the system. If she filed a complaint, she would be back behind bars by day's end. Too much about this fucked-up system works against her."

He knew Charlotte wanted to argue, but she lifted her hands and let out a rough sigh. "So what about Eva? I don't want this around her. She's too fragile."

"I hear you, Charlotte, I really do, but Eva is stronger than you think. What's the alternative? Not letting her see Reine? She's old enough to understand something is wrong, so how long do you think it'll be until she starts figuring out we're lying to her, keeping her mother away from her? She'll never forgive us, even though we're doing it to protect her…"

He could see Charlotte wanted to argue with him, but the phone was ringing out front.

"We'll figure it out," he said. "But we're going to have to talk to Reine and work something out."

Charlotte walked out of his office and back to her desk. He could still hear Arnie fussing from the back of the pen as she answered the phone. Maybe he should call Suzanne and thank her for doing what he should have done. Food, shelter… It was just common human decency. Maybe they could take turns. He'd mention it when he saw them at Ryan's on Friday.

As he walked out of his office, Charlotte turned to him with an odd expression.

"Marcus, a call just came in from Pete Peterson at Better Way about a theft," she said. "One of his employees has been accused of stealing from an elderly woman they have a contract with. He said it was Reine…"

As soon as Charlotte said it, his heart sank. He strode back into his office and grabbed his keys from his desk, then fastened his duty belt, thinking of what this would do to Eva.

"Why would she steal something, Marcus?" Charlotte said.

What the hell was he supposed to think? He considering what he'd seen the night before with his family at her place, a woman with nothing, no food, living in a slum, wanting her daughter back.

What was it about the revolving door of prison? Once out, they were right back in. All he could see now for Reine, Eva's mother, was the wall of bars in her future.

"I'll call you later," was all he said before stepping

out of the stationhouse and pulling the door closed. All he could do was wonder why. Why would she do it?

When he pulled up in front of Better Way, he took in Suzanne standing outside with a woman her height but with a round face, dark skin, and likely fifty pounds on her.

"Suzanne," he said, then glanced at the other woman, standing in front of a dark blue hatchback. He could already feel trouble brewing. "What the hell are you doing here?" he said in a low voice.

Suzanne gestured as if to say she was already neck deep and wasn't going to stay out of anything. "Look, I drove Reine to work, and as I was pulling away, I saw this man come out and start yelling at her. He was screaming, and I could see how scared she was. That kind of anger, he had no right. So I pulled a one-eighty and floored it right back in, jamming the brakes right in front of him. I told him to stop yelling at Reine. Then he starts in about how she's a damn thief and stole from one of their clients, something about missing earrings and jewelry. She's inside now and says she didn't do it."

There was his sister, sticking her nose in police business again.

"I got it from here," he said. "You need to go pick up Arnie from the station and go home. Harold had to bring him to work."

His stubborn sister was ready to dig in and argue with him.

"Please, Suzanne, this isn't the time for you to be stepping into this. Please go. I've got this."

"Marcus, excuse me, but I don't think you do," she said. "This is Reine. How objective are you going to be?"

At times, butting heads with Suzanne was amusing, but now it wasn't.

"Don't tell me how to do my job, Suzanne," he said, knowing it had come out sharper than he wanted. He walked around her and over to the woman still standing there. "Did you call about a theft?" he said.

She shook her head and jabbed her finger at the door. "No, sir, that was Pete. I told him hiring an ex-con was a bad idea. Now look at this mess. You think I want this on my plate? I've got a busy enough day, and now we're down a body and it's me who's going to have to pick up the slack."

Marcus reached for the industrial glass door and pulled it open, taking in the small front waiting area, hearing a man shouting from in back, then what he thought was Reine's voice. He took in two other women in pink scrubs by the counter in front, one with light hair pulled back, on the heavy side, the other tall, thin, dark haired. Both were listening to everything. He was familiar with this kind of energy, walking into a situation.

"Don't go anywhere. I'm going to want to talk to you both," was all he said to them before heading to one of two office doors. It was open, revealing a slender man with thinning dark hair yelling at Reine, who was standing there, gesturing sharply.

He knocked on the open door, and they both looked over to him. He took in the flicker of emotion in Reine's eyes, panic, anger. Then she shut them, and he could see how pale she was. The side of her face showed a hint of bruising and swelling even though he could see she'd tried to cover it with makeup. He hadn't expected that.

"Well, it's about time you got here, Sheriff. I want

her arrested, now." The man stalked toward him, lifting his hand sharply in the air.

"You just step on back there, please," Marcus said, flicking his hand to the man, his other resting on his duty belt. He dragged his gaze back to Reine. "So who wants to tell me what the hell is going on here?"

Reine only crossed her arms and looked away from him.

The man, who he thought had to be Pete, said, "Reine Colbert stole a family heirloom brooch, ruby earrings, and a diamond ring worth over fifty thousand dollars."

"It's not true," Reine said. He could hear the defeat in her voice, and she wouldn't look his way.

"Sheriff, I demand you arrest her. She was the last one at the Hirsts' yesterday when the jewelry went missing. The daughter discovered it last night. She called this morning. Ms. Colbert is already a criminal. Damn it to hell, you little bitch! This is what I get for helping out an ex-con. Everyone told me not to do it, that it would come back to bite me in the ass, and sure enough..." The man was furious.

Marcus lifted his hand when he went to step closer to Reine. "I told you to step back, and I meant it," he said.

The man flicked his hazel eyes toward him, tinged with the kind of fury that could dial up the unease here. "Well, come on now. What are you waiting for? Arrest her!"

Marcus pulled his gaze from the man demanding he do his job to Reine, who had said nothing to defend herself. "Reine, you have to say something. Did you take the jewelry? Were you the last one at the house?" he said without approaching her, seeing how tightly she had pulled her arms across her chest.

She looked over to him. Any hope seemed to have left her, and she shrugged. "Does it really matter? Seems I've already been convicted. Well, I guess you get your wish now, Marcus, and you really will get to keep Eva, keep me out of her life and her away from me." She shrugged once more. "I'll never see her again."

Chapter Twelve

Reine was now sitting in a chair with her hands cuffed behind her back because Pete had demanded Marcus arrest her. She had watched in horror as he pulled his cuffs from his pouch, turned her around, and made her put her hands on her head, fingers linked, as he patted her down and searched her pockets, pulling out her key, the granola bar Suzanne had handed her, and the twelve dollars and twenty-six cents she had left after buying the day-old sandwich. It was all on Pete's desk now, and her pockets were still inside out. Her legs were shaking.

She wondered if they seriously thought she'd be walking around with the old woman's jewelry in her pockets. How the hell had she managed to land in this hot water when she never should have been left alone in the Hirst house anyway? She was Ivy's assistant, doing all the grunt work and dirty jobs the nurses didn't do. Anger was the only emotion going through her now.

This was a nightmare. How? Why? She'd been out of jail for only a week.

She could hear Pete still yelling, feeling the force of his rage in the accusations he yelled down at her. *Where is it? You stupid little fucking bitch. You steal from one of my clients? It's the end of you.* She knew Pete was a friend of Manny's, and she'd expected Manny there instead of Marcus, though, as she pulled in a breath and sat uncomfortably, staring at her things on the desk, she knew it was only a matter of time before he showed up, too.

It was so damn official now, the way Marcus was talking to Pete just outside the office, but Reine had stopped listening to the back and forth. Valerie had called to say the old woman's jewelry had been picked through, but she didn't know where to begin in wondering why. There had to be an explanation.

The old woman carried around that case of jewelry because she had dementia. Reine was still furious with Valerie, her daughter, because she hadn't come back when she said she would, and she'd ended up having to chase an old woman down the street.

Reine wanted to cry from the agony that filled every part of her, but all she could feel now was numbness. Maybe there was a point where her body couldn't take one more thing. She sat there, knowing she was going back to bars and concrete, a tiny cell. And her daughter, Eva… She'd never see her again. It was that thought which had tears slipping down her face and her nose running, and she couldn't even wipe it. She sniffed loudly.

"Come on, Reine. You've got to tell me something. Did you really do this?" Marcus said. She hadn't heard him walk back in. She refused to look up at him and shook her head.

"Does it matter? Seems my word means nothing. Seems it's easy to say I did it because I have a record…"

"You were the last person at her house, and now the jewelry is missing. Are you saying you didn't do it?"

She flinched at the way he snapped, but when she lifted her gaze up to him, she saw empathy despite the disbelief in his voice. She couldn't hide her misery, and she couldn't see him clearly through tear-filled eyes, and that only brought out her anger again, because as he stood there, staring down at her, she could see he'd already convicted her. She made a rude sound, pulling at the cuffs, feeling the ache in her shoulders.

"If I say I didn't do it, would you believe me?"

He just stood there and lifted his gaze, letting out a rough sigh.

She shook her head. "Didn't think so, so what does it matter?"

"What did you do with the jewelry, Reine? What was your plan, to sell it, pawn it? You'd have to know we'd track you down, that you'd get caught. Or was it that you thought no one would notice? Stealing from an old woman?" He reached for her arm and pulled her up. "You know the drill. Get up. You hide it somewhere at your place? What were you planning on doing with the money? You said you wanted Eva back. Was this to pay for the lawyer or something else? We'll take that shithole you live in apart and find it, you know. Come clean. It's the only way this gets easier for you."

The way he talked, she found herself hating everything about him, about who he was. Worse, he had her daughter. But he couldn't make her talk. She was furious at Ivy, too, for leaving her the day before and walking out that door. If only she'd said no, if only she'd walked out. But then what? Getting fired wasn't an option, either, because that would have been another strike against her. Seemed she was damned either way.

"This was so stupid on your part, Reine," he said. "You were out and had a chance to get your life together." He was leading her out of the office, and she could feel eyes on her, burning into her, watching her. She could hear them talking, but she'd stopped listening.

Marcus held her arm and pulled open the door to walk her outside, and there was Suzanne—and Ivy, too. She wanted to spit in her face, something she'd never done to anyone. But the woman had left her and put her in an impossible situation. She made herself look away.

"Marcus, you arrested her?"

It ached deep, hearing the way Suzanne spoke about her.

Marcus pulled open the back door of the cruiser, put his hand on her head, and shoved her in the cramped space before closing the door. She could hear only the muffled sounds of the back and forth between brother and sister, the police radio in the background, as she stared through the black mesh and bars in front of her.

He was the law, the sheriff. She'd felt for so long that she didn't have a voice. How could someone so easily accuse her and be believed when she hadn't done it?

The driver's door opened, and Marcus climbed in and started the car. She knew he was watching her in the rear-view mirror as he backed the police car up and pulled out of the parking lot.

"This isn't helping you, Reine. Did you not think of Eva and how this would hurt her? What happened, you going to jail the first time, shouldn't have happened. You weren't a criminal then, but did being inside turn you into one?"

She pulled in a breath, wanting to tell Marcus right where to go. "If I shouldn't have been in jail the first time, why didn't you do something to get me out? Instead, you let me believe you were good and decent, and, like a fool, I let you adopt my daughter. You're so quick to think the worst of me. But ask yourself if that's because now I can't cause you a problem. This way, I'm no longer a threat to you. I have to wonder, Sheriff, how easy it was. And this jewelry going missing, I think the timing is rather convenient for you."

He lifted a sharp gaze to the rear-view again as he drove, then shook his head. The way his face hardened, she knew she wasn't getting on his good side anytime soon.

"You cuffed me to a chair," he said. "I wasn't the sheriff of this county when you were convicted, but I think you need to give yourself a refresher, Reine. I called my sister to get you out, and she worked your case without cost to you. She swung you a deal that was a miracle at the time, considering the DA wanted to make an example of you. I'm sympathetic, but you broke the law."

She knew she'd pushed the wrong buttons with this man. She could hear the edge of his temper in the way he spoke so sharply.

"Are you trying to say someone is setting you up?" he said. "Don't go laying that at my feet. I can see you want to paint me as a monster, and maybe it would be easier for you to justify hating me. But we love Eva, and she's part of our family. And this, what you're doing, is going to hurt that little girl—*my* little girl, very much. That's entirely on you, Reine. You did this to yourself."

"That's right, Sheriff O'Connell, hero. Wash your hands of it and pass the blame to me. I know what I did then. I was trying to survive with my daughter."

Then there was Tommy, whom she'd thought of too many times since. What if she'd never gone with him?

"Eva will always be my daughter," she continued. "I love her and would never do anything to hurt her. Everything I've done has been for her."

He cursed under his breath, and she knew deep down that it didn't matter what she did, what she said. He'd already made up his mind. What hurt more than anything was how easy it seemed for everyone to assume she was automatically guilty, proof be damned. She lowered her head and shut her eyes, because all she could feel was the dark hole she'd fallen into, and her only way out had been snatched away. Worse, the image she continued to see within the darkness was Marcus O'Connell staring down at her.

Chapter Thirteen

He walked Reine into the station, through the front door, and only shook his head at Charlotte in response to her big eyes as she took in Reine.

"Marcus…" she said.

He just kept walking, spotting Harold holding the baby in one arm and thinking his sister had better have her ass in that car and be on her way back as ordered. Though, at the way she had stared at him and told him to drop dead, he had decided picking a fight with her wouldn't solve anything.

Reine had stopped talking completely as he walked her back to the only interrogation room and took in the bar on the table where they cuffed people under arrest. With Reine, he didn't even know where to begin. Why had she done it?

"Marcus, a word," Harold said as Marcus undid Reine's cuffs.

"Sit down. I'll be right back," he said to her before starting to the door, where he shut his eyes for a second, then turned around and watched her rubbing at her wrists. All he saw was the woman who'd given birth to his daughter. Would she ever wonder about this day and ask why her mother couldn't just keep her head down and her nose clean? Harold was still standing outside the doorway of the interrogation room. There was no window. Reine had refused to sit and look his way.

"Do you want some water or something else?"

She shook her head. "No," she said, curt, short. She wasn't going to make this easy.

He pulled the door closed and locked it from the outside, then took in his deputy, who had handed the baby off to Charlotte. He spotted Therese at her desk, too, her phone to her ear.

"Suzanne called," he said. "Your sister is one step from serving your head up."

He let out a rude noise under his breath, because Suzanne knew how to push every one of them. "She needs to keep her nose out of this. I'm not having her interfering in the Reine situation."

Harold had pulled his arms across his chest. Marcus could see he had something on his mind. "I told her that, but, Marcus, you sure you're the right person to talk to Reine? For you, this is personal."

If it were anyone other than Harold, the look he gave would have had him shutting up and walking away. But not Harold. He was shorter than Marcus, but he just stood his ground and nodded toward the room. "You arrested her? She confess to taking the jewelry?"

Marcus shrugged. "Haven't filed all the charges yet. But you forget I'm the sheriff, and, personal or not, I can be objective here. Didn't find the missing jewelry on her, but I can't see her carrying it around. But she had the opportunity. Her employer said she was last there, and then it went missing. Have Therese get over to her place and take it apart. I'm going to talk with Reine and get her to tell me where it is. Told her to make it easier on herself. Dammit! How am I going to tell Eva? I'll have to have a word with her parole officer…"

"Hold up, Marcus," Harold said. "This is Eva's mother, you're right about that, so you can't be the one to go in there and interrogate her. It's bad enough that you showed up for the call and arrested her. With the anger between you two, she's not going to be too forthcoming. If it were the other way around, you'd be telling me exactly the same thing. In this, you can't take the lead, because of Eva."

Marcus was already shaking his head. He was furious Reine would do this and Eva would have to hear her mom was going back to prison. This would hurt his daughter.

"At least let me do the talking and take the lead," Harold said. When Marcus pulled in a breath, Harold seemed to take that as his cue. "Therese," he called out to the newest deputy, who leaned back in her chair, "get a warrant to search Reine Colbert's place. Reach out to her parole officer, and then get over there. You have a list of what we're looking for?"

Marcus pulled out his small notebook, seeing the old woman's name, her address, and the description of the missing items. "Ruby earrings, a diamond ring, and a brooch that's apparently over a hundred years old, a family heirloom. They're saying it's all worth fifty thousand."

Therese nodded and reached for the phone. "Okay, on it," was all she said.

Harold tapped his chest with the back of his hand

and only shook his head before stepping past him, reaching for the door, and opening it.

Marcus knew he was right, but he wanted Reine to tell him why she would jeopardize Eva's peace of mind. She had to know now that she'd never see her again.

Reine was still standing when Harold stopped at the table and pulled out her chair, scraping the steel.

"Reine, sit down," he said. "I'm Deputy Waters. I need you to tell me where the jewelry is."

Marcus could see Reine didn't want to listen, but she walked slowly toward the chair, her blue eyes flickering with such hate for him. She sat down, and he could see she was unwilling to talk.

"Do I not have a right to call a lawyer?" she said, looking right at him and then at Harold, who had walked around the table.

"Of course, but as soon as you do, anything I could do to make this easier for you goes away. One of our deputies is already on her way to your place, and your parole officer too. When they find the jewelry, there will be no deal. As we stand, your parole will be revoked, and you'll have to serve out the rest of your sentence, but how much more time is tacked on to it is up to you." Harold had a way of talking that was so matter of fact.

Reine seemed to have pulled into herself as she flicked her gaze over to him. "You love this, don't you? Then you get to tell Eva how her mother screwed up, how she's better off."

Marcus leaned against the wall and pulled his arms over his chest. "You think I'm enjoying this? Let me tell you, there's nothing I dread more than seeing the pain in Eva's eyes, my daughter's eyes, over what you've done. I don't know how to tell her. I don't want to tell her.

Why would you do this, Reine? You had to know I would've worked something out with you. I wouldn't have completely cut you out of her life…"

"Oh, you are such a liar, Marcus O'Connell—or, excuse me, Sheriff." Her tone was overly sarcastic, laced with a ton of disrespect. "The only intention you had was to keep me away from my daughter. What exactly did you say when I showed up at your door? No! You said it wasn't going to happen, and when my daughter wanted me to show up to your mother's house last night, you waited until your wife got her out of the house before telling me I wasn't to go. What was the exact word, uninvited? So excuse me if I don't believe a word you say." She leaned forward, then sat straight.

By the way she carefully looked over at Harold, he wondered whether she expected something else to come at her. He could still see the bruising on her face, the swelling underneath the makeup that had worn off.

"Reine, we are way past that," he said. "I guess at this point it doesn't matter what you believe. Is that why you helped yourself to someone's jewelry? Was the plan to pawn it? You have to know we're going to look, and we will find it. Pawn shops have security footage." Well, most did. Some had cameras that conveniently didn't work.

She pressed her lips together, digging in. "So is that a no to my request for a lawyer? Let's be clear here, cards on the table. I already told you I didn't take the jewelry, but it seems you've convicted me. I can't understand how quick you were to take the word of someone who pointed the finger my way. I have a record, but I've never stolen anything in my life. And what really infuriates me is that I was never even supposed to be left alone in that home. I was the slave who did all the dirty work the nurses don't, cleaning up soiled adult diapers, scrubbing the bathtub and the floor. Apparently, that's all I'm good for.

"But I was never meant to be in the house without Ivy, the nurse I was assigned to. I was to leave with her and show up with her, not be told to stay and clean because she was done when I still had way more to do. Then I had to chase a woman with dementia down the street because her daughter never came home. I had to stay hours after I was supposed to be off, and I'll never get paid for it, and now I'm suddenly accused of taking jewelry. Really?" She kept looking his way instead of at Harold, who was perched on the edge of the table, looking down at her.

The deputy dragged his gaze to Marcus, who knew that look. She'd said it enough times, asking for a lawyer, so they had to listen.

"You can have a lawyer," Marcus said, "but as soon as you get your lawyer and we're done here, there's no negotiating something better for you."

She flicked her gaze up to Harold. Marcus couldn't remember ever having seen the kind of determination that was on her face now. She stood up and held her arms out in front of her, saying, "Take me to my cell, because I'm not talking again. I told you the truth, and you don't believe me. We're done. I have nothing to say to you."

Harold stood up and looked Marcus's way. There was nothing more they could do, so Marcus put his hand on the door and pulled it open, then tossed over his shoulder to Harold, "Let her call her lawyer. Then charge her."

Chapter Fourteen

He took in Manny, who was standing just outside the open door to Reine's basement suite, as he pulled up and parked on the street. The door was wide open, and Harold had just walked through it. He knew Therese was already inside.

There were a lot of cars in front of the rundown rental, and with two cop cars added to the mix, it was only reasonable that people were watching from the suite above Reine's. It was quite the show, a situation he walked into far too often.

The whispers, the watching. God damn, he hated it.

He turned off his car, feeling the weight of his office and the daggers Suzanne had glared at him. All he'd said to her when she walked into his station was "Stay out of it." He wasn't a monster, but he didn't like his integrity being questioned.

His phone was ringing, and he pressed answer. "O'Connell," he snapped, closing the door of his car and stepping onto the dry brown grass.

"I just got a very angry call from our sister," Karen

said. "Well, actually, Jack did, because I was in a meeting. He had to pull me out because Suzanne was demanding your head on a platter. I've never heard her so angry, Marcus. What the hell is going on, and why is Reine in jail?"

He really didn't want to deal with another angry sister right now. "It's an active investigation, Karen, so this isn't the time to stick your nose into this."

"Oh, cut the crap, Marcus. Did you seriously arrest Reine? What is this about her being accused of theft? Suzanne said she was accused of stealing jewelry. Did she really?"

He shook his head. Everything about this situation had him on edge, and having his sisters questioning him was really beginning to piss him off. "She'll be charged with felony theft along with exploitation of a vulnerable person, so this is damn serious. Her parole officer is here already, and her place is being searched now. I don't understand why she did it. Was it to get Eva back? She may not have been a criminal before she went into prison, but she sure is now. Look, I've got to go."

"No, Marcus, wait. You're really throwing the book at her? What has the DA said?"

He didn't want to do this with Karen. "Do you not understand the part about us still investigating? As soon as we locate the stolen jewelry, the DA can weigh in, but I guarantee you my office will not be lenient, and the DA certainly won't, especially for a repeat offender. There's no deal. She'll get the maximum plus whatever else they decide to throw at her. When she gets out next time, I won't have to worry about her showing up at the door, because Eva will be in her twenties and not a little girl anymore, with a life of her own, and Reine will be an old woman…"

At first, there was silence on the other end. "Did Reine confess?" Karen finally said. "Did you find the jewelry?"

"Are you asking as her lawyer or my sister?"

She hissed, likely from how sharply it had come out.

He was now two steps from Manny, who was standing outside the door, appearing both indignant and furious. Every time he looked at the man only reinforced how much he really disliked him.

"You know what, Marcus?" Karen said. "There's a side of you I don't like, and this is it. I remember once upon a time, a young, stupid Marcus O'Connell stole and got into all kinds of trouble, yet here you are now, unscathed, and with a badge. Amazing, once the shoe is on the other foot…"

He could feel her nastiness coming out, and he stopped walking, turning away from Manny. "Okay, I think we're done," he said, cutting his sister off. He actually pressed the end button and hung up before she could add one more dig at his character. This wasn't about him. This was about a woman who'd been given a chance and blown it.

Marcus shoved his phone in his pocket. His empathy for a woman who'd been through hell only added to the fury burning inside him. For liars, he wasn't prepared to be lenient, but maybe because this was Eva's mother, he was struggling with a dark moodiness, furious at how it seemed everyone was trying to make him the bad guy.

He made himself turn around and take another step until he was in front of Manny.

"Well, how about I say I told you so?" was the first thing out of Manny's mouth.

Marcus took in his dingy dress shirt, the sleeves rolled up, and what looked like the same brown pants he always wore. He had to remind himself that his mood wasn't winning him any points today, but he took another second to stare down at the man and his pale face, the heavy bags under eyes that stared back at him with a kind of self-righteousness.

"Sure, you could do that," Marcus said, "or maybe you could explain what happened to Reine's face, the bruising from the fist that landed there." He settled his stance, his hands on his duty belt.

The man didn't even flinch. "I don't know, Sheriff. Maybe she got herself into a situation. Wouldn't be surprised if some john rolled her."

Marcus couldn't believe the man had said it with such a straight face. "Unbelievable," he muttered under his breath, knowing that if it were anyone else, another ex-con instead of Reine, he'd likely have believed him.

He took in the open door, hearing the voices and rustling inside. If he stood there and listened to the piece of shit in front of him, nothing good would come out of his mouth in response. His sound reasoning, which was hanging on by a thread, would be gone. So he made himself walk into the basement suite, seeing groceries on the counter, cans of food, cheese, lettuce, sandwich meat, and milk that Harold had pulled from the tiny fridge. His sister really had stepped up, and maybe it was the guilt that was making him so angry. He should have been the one to show up with groceries.

The cupboards were open, the drawers, and a box of cereal had been dumped out in a large plastic bowl.

A cell phone was next to it in a plastic bag. Harold had pulled the mini fridge away from the wall and was looking behind it.

Marcus strode over to him. "Anything?"

Harold only shook his head. "Nothing. Therese has gone through every nook in the bathroom, the bedroom…"

Marcus took in the sofa cushions, which had been unzipped and the foam pulled out.

"I hate to say this, but it's not here," Harold said. "Check the pawn shops. This happened yesterday, so maybe there's some footage. But nothing here." He stood up and opened the carton of eggs, then put them back in the emptied fridge.

Marcus gestured to the small suite, trying to piece it together, the timing, given when his family had shown up. Then there was her parole officer. "Manny, get in here," he called out. "What time did you show up here yesterday?"

He knew Harold was watching the man too as he stepped inside.

"Sheriff, nothing is here," said Therese, who stepped out of the tiny bedroom in her brown deputy uniform, her dark hair cut short,. He didn't miss the way she stared over at Manny, saying nothing but not pulling any punches in the disgust she leveled his way.

Marcus took in the small suite. There weren't many places to hide something. "Head over to the Hirsts', and this time see if you can get a photo of the jewelry Reine took," he said to Therese. "I want statements, too. Don't miss anything. I want a written formal statement from the daughter, and talk to the mother, too, if you can."

"You mean the mother with dementia?"

Marcus pulled in a breath. "Yeah."

Therese made a face, then said, "Yes, Sheriff," as she started to the door. Manny was forced to step out of her way, but as he let his gaze flicker over her and down, Marcus knew there could be a problem there.

Manny was looking out the door, evidently still watching Therese, when Marcus said, "Manny, I asked you about yesterday. You showed up here at what time?"

The man hesitated, then dragged his gaze over to Marcus. He wondered if he was trying to piece together a story, because he gave nothing away in his expression. "An after-work visit, not long after she got home, likely five thirtyish, sixish. Don't know the exact time, but there was plenty of time for her to stash or pawn what she lifted. You know well, Sheriff, that if it's not here, that doesn't mean she didn't take it. She could've already pawned it off or sold it on the streets."

Marcus pulled in a breath. A hundred different scenarios could have happened. If she was smart, she wouldn't have brought the stolen jewels back here anyway. She could have hidden them anywhere. He didn't believe Reine was stupid by any means. He looked down to Harold, who hadn't pulled his gaze from Manny.

"There're a couple of pawn shops not far from here," Harold said in a low voice as he turned from the man. "I'll take a ride over."

Marcus nodded, then glanced around at the suite that had been taken apart and the food he knew his sister had bought. "Let me know what you find out," he said.

Harold seemed to hesitate, then glanced back over to

Manny, that heavy all-cop gaze he had when he was figuring out a suspect.

"I'll close up here," Marcus said, knowing Harold understood he wasn't done.

"What a waste," Manny said. "Well, if it's all the same to you, Sheriff, I have a full caseload. I'll notify the warden and the parole board…"

"Just a minute, Manny. I want a word with you." Marcus took a step, and Harold evidently took that as his cue, as he started walking to the door, moving past Manny in the cramped entryway.

Marcus moved the tiny fridge back against the wall and pulled it open to stuff in the bag of lettuce, cheese, sandwich meat, and milk. He heard Manny reach for a paper bag folded on the counter, and he started tucking the unopened groceries, cans, box of granola bars, cereal, pasta, and jars of sauce into it.

"What are you doing?" Marcus said.

Manny tossed him an odd glance over his shoulder. "She has no use for these groceries."

"Yeah, well, you're not helping yourself to them. I want to talk to you about your visit to Reine. What exactly went on here, and how was it that when I showed up after with my family, this place had been torn apart and she appeared as if she'd just been hit? You think I don't know you hit her? Punching a woman, is that what you did? You get off on that, Manny?"

The man froze before tucking the spaghetti sauce into the bag as if he had no intention of listening to Marcus. Then he slowly turned, and the way his brow knit and his eyes darkened, Marcus could already feel the spin he was planning.

"I was doing my job, Sheriff," he said. "If I recall,

you're the one who paid me a visit and brought me up to speed on the shenanigans of my parolee. How I handle my parolees is not your concern or your business."

Marcus wondered whether the rough laugh he let rumble under his breath was enough of a warning that he wasn't in the mood for games. "You hitting a woman is my business."

"Who said I hit her?" Manny was loud and actually lifted his hands up rather dramatically. "Already told you it was likely some john."

"Really, so was this before or after you arrived?"

The man just stared at him and pulled in a breath, thinking. He let the seconds tick.

"I don't recall," Manny said. "You know, the number of times I see this…"

"And you don't report it? Now, why don't I believe that?"

The parole officer only shook his head, then reached for the bag of groceries. The prick was actually going to walk out the door with them!

Marcus flicked his hand to him. "Put it down. You're not taking that. Word of advice, Manny. If I ever hear of you putting your hands on another woman, I will make your life a living hell. You seem to think that because Reine is in the trouble she is, with a record and the label of ex-con, you can do whatever you want to her, terrorize her, brutalize her, and she has to take it. But let me be clear: I will break you, and then I will take apart your life, and my deputies will spend their days talking to every single parolee you have and have ever had, every past relationship you've been in. I will uncover every piece of dirt on you, and I will bury you. Do we understand each other?"

As Manny put the paper bag of groceries down and stepped back and over to the door, Marcus tracked his every move. The man said nothing, then stopped in the open doorway and looked back to him.

"You know, Sheriff, you don't get it. You have no idea what it's like to work with ex-cons who are always up to no good, spinning some lie, some story. You know that convict who got out of jail is going to hurt someone, or steal from someone, or do something bad, and then the spotlight will be shining down on me, the parole officer, with hard questions about why I didn't figure out and catch him or stop him. She's just one more who's lost her rights. Don't forget how the law works, Sheriff. She's an ex-con. You want to know her record from prison, the fights she was in or started, or the trouble she caused?"

Marcus just took in the man he couldn't believe actually served as a gateway for those getting a chance at a new life. "Don't spin it, Manny, not with me. I want your notes about your visit to Reine's sent over to my office: the time you arrived, how long you were here, and how you tore her place apart. You find anything? I want it all, what you saw, what she said, what you did. You'd better have the times down, too. Are we clear?"

Manny shook his head, standing in the doorway. Even from his profile, Marcus could see the face he made. "Sounds to me like you're more interested in protecting a criminal than an old woman with dementia. Wonder what folks would think if word got out in the community about where the sheriff's priorities really lie. You forget the voting population are the older generation who actually own something." Then Manny walked out of the suite.

"Fucking asshole," Marcus spat out under his breath as he listened to the gravel crunching, knowing that prick of a parole officer was dirty, underhanded, and a snake.

Manny Meskill had never been on his radar before, but Marcus realized he needed to be more careful in what he said to him, in how he looked into his personal and private business. The parole officer wasn't a stupid man, and if Marcus wasn't careful, he could end up on the defensive. A lie could easily be spun, and then Manny Meskill could very well become untouchable.

Chapter Fifteen

Her one phone call had been to Gregor Smith, and his secretary had said he was out of the office on personal business.

Personal business! What the hell did that mean? Likely that no help would be on its way for her, though she'd left a message, of course.

As she stared at the bars of her cell and the concrete surrounding her where she sat on the small cot, her stomach rumbled. She thought of the granola bar that had been in her pocket and was likely now tucked in an envelope with the key and cash Marcus had taken. She kept listening for the door, because it was only a matter of time before she was cuffed again and transported back to prison.

The image of the place she'd hoped to never see again flashed through her head, a life beyond hell, with her cell mate and the other inmates she hoped to never see again. Then there were the guards, who she knew wouldn't welcome her with open arms.

She was leaning against the wall, her feet propped

up on the cot, when she heard the door and then footsteps. She slid her feet to the floor, and her heart thudded. How could she prepare mentally for a life without freedom? She shut her eyes because the ache was too much.

She heard voices and glanced over to see Karen O'Connell. Her hair was dark with a few highlights of red and blond, hanging long and loose, and she wore sandals and a navy sundress, very pregnant. Her hand was on the bars, and the impressive ring on her finger flashed. Reine just stared, her stomach knotting, wondering what was coming next. She said nothing as she stared at a deputy she didn't know standing next to Karen.

"I should ask how you are," Karen said, "but seeing where you are answers that question. Your face, Suzanne said your parole officer did that?" She gestured through the bars.

All Reine did was stare at Karen, her hands curled around the edge of the cot, then drag her gaze to the lanky young light-haired deputy.

"Colby, open it up," Karen said to him, resting her hand over her large baby bump.

"You know Marcus isn't going to like this," Colby said to Karen. Reine listened to the scrape of the bars as he opened her cell.

"Don't you worry about my brother," Karen said, patting the young deputy's shoulder. She stepped inside the cell.

"What is this?" was all Reine could think to ask. She slowly stood up, wondering whether Marcus O'Connell, the sheriff himself, was going to appear next.

"Thanks, Colby. Can you leave us alone, please?"

Colby shook his head. "The sheriff will have my head on a chopping block for this. I shouldn't be letting you back here…"

"Oh, Colby, I'll deal with him," Karen said, now inside the tiny cell.

Reine didn't miss the wide eyes and worried expression on the young deputy's face. Apparently, he didn't want to be on Marcus's bad side, which was exactly where she was. But then he reached back and ran his hand over his head.

"You've got five minutes, that's it, and then you have to go," he said in a low voice, then walked away. She heard the door at the end of the small cell block open and close. Karen pulled in a breath.

Reine didn't have a clue what to say or do. "I don't understand why you're here," she said, standing up and just staring at her. She was Reine's height, and the way she fixed her blue eyes on her confused the hell out of her.

"Do you mind?" Karen gestured to the cot Reine had been sitting on.

"Be my guest," she said.

Karen pressed a hand to her lower back and sat down with a groan. "You call a lawyer yet?" she said, looking up at her.

Reine wondered how much of what she said would go right back to Marcus. "He's away on personal business. Left a message, but not sure when or if I'll hear from him—not that it matters, since I expect to be in prison before the day's out."

Her stomach rumbled again, and Karen flicked her gaze from her face to her stomach and back, then gave her head a shake and said, "Well, then I guess you have me as your lawyer."

She wasn't sure she'd heard right. She pulled her arms over her chest and shook her head. "You realize your brother, the sheriff, wouldn't be happy about that. Honestly, Karen, I appreciate it, but you're still Marcus's sister, his family. You all have my daughter, and before this, you have to know I told Marcus I want Eva back…"

Karen lifted a hand to stop her. "I'm very well aware of your showing up on my brother's doorstep to see Eva and the way you two locked horns, and of what's gone down between the two of you and everything that was said. I also know Marcus probably overreacted, but you have to know my brother would do anything for Eva. He loves that little girl. We all do, Reine. She's part of our family."

Reine only nodded, knowing it was true, but just hearing her daughter's name, knowing what she'd lost, was eating her from the inside out. "So is this why you're here, to toss me something and make sure I stay far away from Eva?" She shook her head. "She's my daughter…"

"I know that." Karen cut her off quite sharply. "No one is trying to cut you out, but, Reine, the situation you're in right now is dire. You're being charged with felony theft, and with the missing jewelry being valued over fifty thousand, that kind of charge will easily tack another ten years onto your sentence. Your parole will be revoked, too, and you'll have to serve out the remainder of your other sentence as well, because there will be no deal."

She only nodded, thinking of the parole officer who

hated her, of Pete, her boss, who had scared the hell out of her, and of Ivy, who had left her alone with Mrs. Hirst. Most of all, she thought of the voice she had lost.

"I didn't take any jewelry," she said. "How is it so easy to say I did something when I didn't? I'm not a stupid woman, Karen, but there's a point when you have no rights that no one listens to you. Someone has said I did something and is pointing the finger, based on what? Did they find the jewelry on me? I expect they already searched my place, and there's nothing there. Yet I half expect Marcus—excuse me, Sheriff O'Connell, to walk in here and hold up the evidence that he found it. Sure would be an easy way to get rid of me, wouldn't it?"

She didn't know what to make of the expression on Karen's face, the way her jaw slackened and she let out a breath as if she couldn't figure out what to say. Reine expected her to get up and leave. After all, family was family. But instead she looked away and shook her head, an odd expression on her face.

"I hear you, Reine. But the anger you have for Marcus is misplaced. He would never plant evidence. I can tell by the way you're looking at me that you don't believe me. Will they find something that shouldn't be there, Reine? I think you know what I'm talking about."

She thought of her cell phone, the one she'd hidden in the box of cereal. She still couldn't understand why she hadn't been able to shake the need to hide it.

"Other than the burner cell I bought, which I tucked into a box of crispy rice cereal…"

Karen lifted her brows. "Why would you hide a cell phone?"

How was she supposed to explain her irrational fear, having to hide everything, being allowed nothing?

"Because a cell phone isn't allowed in prison, even though there were inmates who had them, you know, the ones who run things from the inside with the help of the guards. I know it's not rational, but I can't just wake up one morning and suddenly act normal. I'm scared all the time, and maybe it's paranoia, I don't know, but being told over and over that I have no rights and that anyone can take anything from me at any time…" She didn't think she'd get her to understand. She let out a weary sigh and lifted her hands, because just saying it out loud sounded so crazy.

"Okay, all right, let's just park that thought and back up," Karen said. "So other than the cell phone tucked in a box of cereal, what else is there?"

Reine shook her head. "Your sister, Suzanne, showed up with food this morning, but there's nothing else. You know, what makes me so angry is that I didn't even want to stay in that house. The nurse I work under left me there and told me to stay and wait for the daughter to come home after giving me a list of everything to clean. I wasn't supposed to be there alone. The old woman has dementia. Did you know I had to run up the street after her because she walked out the door? Her daughter, Valerie, didn't come home when she was supposed to, at two. It was after four when she walked back through the door, and I was so damn angry at her, and she had to know. How can you get anything done while keeping an eye on an old woman who can't look after herself? I didn't see this coming. But Mrs. Hirst asked me to help her with a pearl necklace, so I put it on her. She had this box of jewelry…"

"So your prints will be on the jewelry?" Karen cut in.

Reine shrugged, trying to remember every moment of that day. She wished she could go back and do... what, argue with Ivy, tell her no? Then she'd have been fired, another mess, a different parole violation.

"My prints will be all over the house, and on the pearl necklace for sure. But why is the finger being pointed at me? I don't have the jewelry. Could the old woman have put it somewhere? Did anyone look in the house? She stashed things, you know, especially her soiled adult diapers. I found them in the oddest of places, behind the toilet, in the back of the cupboards under the sink in the bathroom, in the hall closet when I was getting clean towels, under her bed... Maybe this missing jewelry is there?" She pressed her hands over her face and pulled them down. "How is it, Karen, that someone can accuse me of stealing? Where is the jewelry?"

Karen rested her hand over the baby she carried. Seeing her like that reminded Reine of when she'd carried Eva, how happy she and Vern had been. Another lifetime, one in which she had no idea anyone could be treated so horribly.

"Unfortunately, it happens too often, Reine. You can be charged, depending on the circumstances and who accused you of the theft. With your record and your being on parole, unfortunately, you won't be believed, because in the eyes of the law, you have to prove your innocence. The person accusing you has status and credibility in the community. The law is usually grey, not black and white. But let me find out what's going on. Let's get these charges dropped. But hear me on this, Reine: They could transport you back to prison and revoke your parole even if we manage to get this dropped."

Karen struggled to edge off the cot and stand up, and Reine stepped closer and held out her hand. Karen hesitated only a second before slipping her hand into hers and letting her help her to her feet.

"So when is the baby due?"

A smile tugged at her lips. "Five more weeks, give or take." Karen reached over and ran her hand over her shoulder. "Hang in there, Reine. Don't talk to anyone," she said, then flicked her gaze to Reine's face. She knew she was staring at the bruising, which had been a constant stiff ache. She lifted a hand, and Reine thought she was going to touch it, but she pulled her hand away. "And just know, too, that I plan on nailing the asshole who hit you. He can't get away with it."

Reine pulled in a deep breath and stared at Karen. "Don't you understand? He already has."

Karen glanced at the open door of the cell and then looked back at her. "Reine, I get why you say that, but a man like him, this isn't a one-time thing. He'll have done this before, and he believes he's untouchable."

"It's my word against his. Don't forget who he is and who I am."

Karen groaned, and it sounded like frustration. She stepped out of the cell. "I'll have some food sent back to you. Any requests?"

There was just something about Karen O'Connell that she remembered fondly. The woman was a pit bull, and she made Reine feel as if she mattered.

"Anything is fine, thank you."

Karen nodded and stepped out of the cell, her hand on the bar, about to close it. "Don't lose faith, Reine. I know you have issues with Marcus, but when this is all over, we really do need to sit down and talk about Eva."

She sensed she was about to be warned off. "Are you asking me to walk away from my daughter in exchange for helping me?"

Karen reminded her of Marcus in some ways, like how she looked over to her with a flicker of fire in her eyes. "I would never do that. One doesn't cancel out the other. Reine, no one is asking you to walk away from Eva. You're still her mother, but we're her family, too."

Then she tapped the bars, pulled the cell door closed with a clatter, and, with a final look to her, walked away. Reine heard the door at the end open and close, and she strode over to the cot and sat down, feeling for the first time that maybe, just maybe, someone was in her corner.

Chapter Sixteen

Marcus's cell phone was ringing again, but he ignored it. He couldn't remember the last time he'd had such a dark cloud hanging heavy over him, having him snapping at everyone.

He parked in front of a pawn shop in the center of town and took in the car parked next to him, which looked an awful lot like Harold's Kia. He stepped out of his sheriff's cruiser and spotted Harold's cruiser parked on the other side of the Kia. He was already shaking his head, seeing the baby car seat and the diaper bag.

"Fuck!"

The breath he pulled in did nothing to cool the fire in his belly, which had him wanting to yell and wring his sister's neck. She was really stepping into his business, and he wasn't going to stand for it.

He pulled off his shades and tucked them in his shirtfront before yanking harder than he normally would on the commercial glass front door of the pawn shop. Harold was standing there with Suzanne, who had his nephew snuggled in a baby carrier she was wearing. She rocked from side to side, patting his bottom, and the minute her eyes locked on to his, he could feel she was ready to go another round. It was just something about her face. He wondered whether she had any idea of the way her lips pulled back to show her teeth. He could see the snarl just for him.

He let himself take in the shop, the large man behind the glass counter with a heavy white beard and unsmiling dark expression. Marcus said nothing as he lifted his gaze to Harold, who had the lost look he knew only Suzanne could put on his face.

"You need to take your wife home," he said. He knew he was going down a road that could have him and Suzanne on the outs, but he wasn't in the mood to play nice with her. He stopped right in front of Suzanne, looking down at her. "I'm not kidding, Suzanne. I want you out of here now."

"This is a free country, and neither of you can tell me what to do. So get that through your head right now," she said.

Marcus took a step closer and leaned down to Suzanne, then said in a low voice, "Don't push me." He really emphasized the words and could feel the fire blazing in his eyes.

Suzanne didn't flinch, though, and he knew her stubborn streak well. She would really dig in and stand her ground. He stepped back and took in Harold, who angled his head as if he had something to say as well.

"You find anything? Was she here?" Marcus said.

"As I was just telling your deputy, my husband," Suzanne said, "before you walked in here throwing your weight and arrogance around, I've already talked to the owner. Hey, Randall, can you tell these two what you told me about the jewelry I was asking about?" she called out over her shoulder to the big man behind the counter.

She really was stepping into it. He was about to reach for his sister's arm and walk her out of the pawn shop when the heavyset man, who didn't appear as if he ever smiled, shrugged.

"Jewelry doesn't often make its way in here, but every time someone asks, I send them next door to the jewelry store," he said. "If you're looking for quick cash, I offer only twenty, thirty percent of value, but Lowes jewelry store consigns all the time, and the markup…" He gestured wide.

Marcus just stared. This wasn't what he'd expected, and, worse, he could feel the smugness of his sister's gaze burning into him, likely gloating. He knew she expected him to say "Way to go, Suzanne!" but there was no way in hell he would. He fought the urge to look at her.

"You talk to them next door?" he said to Harold, whose large arms were crossed over his chest, his gaze lingering on Suzanne.

"Not yet. I got here just before you…"

Suzanne cleared her throat. "Randall, do you want to tell them about the woman who came in here, inquiring how much you would give her for a brooch that had diamonds and emeralds, an antique one? You said it was pretty rare."

His jaw tightened, and he flicked his gaze to his sister, who was standing firmly in police business. He reached for her arm, and her gaze flicked right to his hand as he said, "Come over here," and moved them back so they were out of hearing range of the guy behind the counter.

"Hands off, Marcus," Harold said in a low warning voice he hadn't heard before. Then he shot his wife a hard glance and said, "And you, stop butting heads with Marcus. Whether you like it or not, Suzanne, Marcus is the sheriff, and this is an active investigation. You're not a cop."

"But I'm the one—"

"Uh-uh," Harold cut in. Whatever passed between them, Marcus realized maybe Harold actually could get through to his pigheaded, stubborn sister. "Suzanne, I get that you want to help, but this isn't helping."

"Really? Because both of you have tunnel vision. Are you not even interested in the woman, the brooch? I was standing there, listening to the jerk who runs Better Way Homecare yelling about the missing jewelry, ruby earrings, a diamond ring, and a brooch that had been in the family a long time. You don't seem even the least bit curious that Randall has now told me about an antique brooch that was worth something. That isn't an everyday occurrence. I mean, how many people have something like that?"

Marcus shook his head and stepped around Suzanne over to Randall, who stood there, watching them. He wore a navy T-shirt, and his weight filled a pair of blue jeans. His eyes were an odd shade of brown.

"You had a woman come in here with a brooch, an antique?"

The man hesitated, and for a second, he wasn't sure he would answer. Maybe it was cops he didn't want to talk to. "As I told Suzanne, I don't see things like that walk through this door. It was a solid fifteen karats, rare beyond belief. I'm not a jeweler, but with the stones, diamond and emerald, it was worth something. I told the lady I wouldn't give her anywhere near what it's worth, so if she needed quick cash, I could give her five hundred, but then I'd consign it next door at Lowes, and I'd likely get a few thousand, easy. Could be more. I gave her the option, and she thanked me and left. I can only assume she went next door to consign it."

Marcus didn't pull his gaze. "So it was just a brooch, no earrings, or a diamond ring? She came in when?" He took in the glass case in front of him, which held a number of expensive watches, a trumpet, and antique revolvers. He looked up for the camera on the wall.

"Yesterday, don't remember exactly when, and she only asked about a brooch. If she had other jewelry, she didn't say, because she left and, as I said, likely went next door."

So Reine had tried to pawn it.

"You know who this woman was? Could you identify her? I know you have cameras." He angled his head at the one on the wall behind Randall and wondered if the man would lie to him. Marcus walked down the case, seeing some gentlemen's rings, some gold cases, an old flask, cameras, and a guitar behind the cabinet—an assortment of things.

"Don't think she was that old, dark hair, light eyes. Camera's been on the fritz, so I can't help you there. As I said, I didn't buy any jewelry."

Marcus took in the camera mounted on the wall again and its position to the door, to any customers who walked in and talked to him. Again, he took in the watches and gentleman's rings in the front case. "So you never buy jewelry?"

The man wasn't quick to answer but didn't look away. Marcus always knew when someone was hiding something, and anyone coming into a pawn shop had sunk to desperation and was likely hiding something.

"I didn't buy her brooch, but she looked desperate, not the typical shithead that walks in here. I felt for her. Didn't say I don't buy jewelry, as you can see. But, again, I offer way below value. What you see here is the result of someone needing fast cash for rent, food, then hoping to buy it back."

"Buy it back, with this kind of markup? That would work out to more than a hundred percent interest, right? But let's talk about the stolen items and the fact that you're supposed to report anything you bring in. Are you telling me everything I see here has been reported to us?"

The man sighed and pulled open a drawer behind him to lift out an old binder, which he dropped on the counter. As he pulled out a sheet of paper, a hand-written list, and held it out, Marcus noted he'd said as little as possible.

"The list up to yesterday," Randall said. "And just FYI, Sheriff, stolen items are sold online these days, not at pawn shops."

Marcus reached for the paper and flicked his gaze up. "You know you're required to have a working camera."

Randall only inhaled. Marcus couldn't remember having dealt with him before and knew he wasn't going to volunteer anything.

"Have it operating by end of day," he warned, then walked over to Harold, taking in his pissed-off sister with the baby in the snuggly. Marcus held out the paper to Harold. "Give this to Colby. See that he checks the database, too. I'm going next door. Seems Reine did come in here. She lied right to my face, damn her."

He kept walking to the door, Harold behind him, followed by his sister, and they stood out on the sidewalk, taking in the jewelry store next to the pawn shop, diamond rings glittering in the window.

"And I don't believe him for one second about the camera," he said. "Get the footage, take a look at it, and find out what he's hiding."

Suzanne, to her credit, said nothing.

Marcus shook his head as he looked at her. "Go home," he said. "I can see you're furious at me over this situation with Reine. You think I don't feel for her? But she did it, and this isn't helping. She's going back to jail. She made the choice to steal from a vulnerable old woman, and it doesn't get any lower than that, in my eyes."

"Marcus…"

"Randall described her, dark hair, light eyes, not that old. You already heard that. I'm going in the jewelry store next, but you need to stop challenging me, Suzanne. Go home, please. No one is happy about this, but the last thing I want to be doing is butting heads with you over Reine, because it's killing me that I have to find the words to tell my little girl, Eva, that her mother is back in prison because she stole something. So this here, with you, I don't want it." He knew he sounded like an asshole, and he flicked his gaze over to Harold, who was about ready to step in between them.

Marcus turned and walked into the jewelry store, seeing the many glass cases.

An older woman in a pencil skirt and a white frilly

blouse smiled and reached out to him. "Sheriff, what can I do for you?"

He took in the glitter of the place and gestured with his thumb in the direction of the pawn shop. "Looking for some stolen jewelry. Was told by the pawn shop owner next door that a woman came in yesterday, dark hair, trying to sell off a brooch. He indicated you do consignment, and he sent her over here?"

Her brow knit, and he wondered whether the big O of her mouth was panic or surprise. "Well, yes, I do consignment on jewelry if it's of value. You said a brooch?"

He stared at the rings, the necklaces, the stones, knowing he'd never be able to afford most things there. "Yes. Did a woman come in here yesterday, dark hair, short, about yay high?" He gestured about how tall Reine was.

The slender older lady walked in heels down to the end of the counter and shoved a key into the lock to open it. "Are you telling me it's stolen?"

He nodded, seeing she wasn't smiling anymore as she pulled a tray of jewelry out and set it on the glass top.

"Yesterday afternoon, a woman said she needed to sell off her jewelry, a brooch that had been in her family a long time. It's fifteen karat gold, Georgian, rare, not something we see often. With the cut of the diamonds, the emeralds, I told her she could get likely six or seven thousand. The earrings were worth not as much, pushing three thousand, maybe…"

"She had earrings too? Ruby, by any chance?"

She flicked her gaze up to him and pulled out a second tray, then pointed to earrings with pear-shaped rubies. "She had a ring, too. I told her it would fetch close to thirty-five thousand."

Whoa!

That was exactly what he didn't want to hear. Reine's fate was sealed, and he didn't know how he could explain this to Eva.

"So it's stolen?" she said. "I didn't see that coming, I suppose you'll need to take them?

He didn't miss the edge in her voice, the same frustration he was feeling. "Yeah, sorry, it will be evidence." He reached into his pocket and pulled out a baggy, then gestured to a tissue box. "Can you hand me a tissue?"

She held out the box, her face questioning, and Marcus pulled out a tissue and used it to pick up the brooch, the earrings, and the glittery diamond ring and toss them in the bag. "Keeping my prints off. I'll send one of my deputies down to lift your prints, too. I'll need you to come down to the station and give a statement. The DA will need it for the charges."

"Any chance I will get my money back?"

He held the bag and stared at the woman. "Money? You gave her money?"

The woman shrugged. "Yes, I advanced her a thousand dollars on the consignment. She was desperate." She opened a drawer behind her and pulled out a big book, which she slid around so he could see the name, signature, and amount.

He took in the log of a thousand dollars and the signature. "The name you have down here…" He put his finger under the black lettering, and the older woman angled her head.

"Valerie Donnelly," she said, nodding, and Marcus just stared at her.

"You said her name was Valerie, not Reine Colbert?"

The woman pulled a face. "She wrote her name down and signed. Is there a problem?"

He reminded himself to breathe in as he considered what he was looking at. So she'd used a different name. She'd been thinking. He glanced back to the door, seeing Suzanne and Harold talking in front of the Kia. He turned back to the woman he thought owned the shop. "You don't by any chance have a surveillance camera, do you?"

She pointed behind her right shoulder. "Sure do, Sheriff. It even works."

"That's good, because I'm going to need to see the footage of this woman."

She nodded and gestured to him. "Okay, you can do that just as soon as you come back with a warrant."

Chapter Seventeen

"Get me a warrant for the Lowes surveillance footage. She was here. It appears she was going to get a tidy sum, and she was apparently advanced a thousand dollars." He held up the plastic bag of jewelry to show Harold, who had his hand on the hood of the Kia as Suzanne tucked Arnie, whom he could hear fussing, into the car seat.

"You want me to take this and log it in as evidence?"

Suzanne closed the back door and headed toward him, conflicted, likely not wanting to believe Reine could have done it. "That makes absolutely no sense, Marcus. Are you sure it was her? You have to be wrong. There has to be another explanation."

He dragged his gaze back to Harold, because it appeared his sister was one step from walking into the jewelry store he'd just walked out of. Taking no was not something she did well.

"Look, Suzanne, I get your frustration, but the evidence is right here, and you already heard the description from Randall in the pawn shop, and the same from the jewelry store. We only need to verify it with security footage. It'll be the final nail, so to speak. Reine's going back to prison for a long time, and she has no one to blame but herself. The food you bought for her is still in the suite, by the way. I'll send Colby to pack it up for you and bring it back."

Suzanne only shut her eyes, then did something he hadn't expected. She walked over to Harold and kissed him, then pulled open the door to the Kia. He wasn't sure what she was going to say, but he could see she was having a hard time wrapping her head around it.

"Call me later?" Suzanne said to Harold, who only nodded and said, "I will."

She slid into the Kia and started it, and he looked back to Harold, who gestured to the plastic bag again.

"You heading back to the station?" he said.

Marcus took in the bag, knowing a lot of Ts still needed to be crossed. There were statements to take, paperwork to do. "Not yet. I'm going to head over to the Hirsts'. Therese should still be there. I'll get her to identify the jewelry and get their reports filed. You get a warrant for that footage—and call Colby, too. When someone starts asking for a warrant, I just get a feeling the camera footage could disappear. So get him down here and inside the store until that warrant shows up. Then I want the footage. You know, I have half a mind to have another go at Reine, show her the jewelry, and get her confession. Sure would make it easier to wrap this up."

Harold said nothing, pulling his solid arms, pure muscle, across his chest. "I'll get the warrant and tell Colby to sit on this place," he said. He headed to his police cruiser but stopped as he pulled open the door.

"What about Better Way Homecare, the boss, and that nurse Reine was working with? You know, the thing that really bothers me about this, Marcus, is something Reine said. She was never supposed to be there alone. Now, I'm not saying it's an excuse, but what does that say about the business, knowingly leaving an ex-con in a house with a vulnerable woman?"

He knew what Harold was saying and wondered if that was what bothered him most out of all of this. "It's not a crime to be a shithead employer, but I do plan on speaking with the nurse she worked under. Better yet, I think I may have her come to the station, sit her down in the interrogation room, and find out if this sort of thing is common practice. It should never have happened." He shook his head.

Harold said nothing else, just got behind the wheel and pulled out.

Marcus tucked the bag of jewelry onto the seat beside him and started his cruiser, staring at the front door of Lowes. He backed out just as his cell phone started ringing again, and he took in the caller ID, Karen Curtis, another sister he didn't want to go a round with. His finger didn't even hover over the green answer icon, instead going right to the red decline.

"Not talking to you right now, Karen," he said to himself, but his phone rang again. This time it was the stationhouse. "Charlotte, what's going on?"

"Your sister is here right now, and she's furious, Marcus, because Manny Meskill has shown up with prison transport, barking orders. They're trying to take Reine back to prison as we speak. I've never seen your sister so angry, and that parole officer… Marcus, I really don't like him. He walked in here with prison transport guards, and they took right over. He handed me an order signed by a judge. Her parole is revoked. They ordered Colby to turn Reine over. Marcus, can they do this?"

He could hear the anxiety and worry in his wife's voice, and he shook his head. He'd known this was coming, but not like this. And Karen was suddenly there? His family were shoving their noses in, which was likely why he wanted to fight them.

"Her parole being revoked is out of my hands, Charlotte. Turn her over. I may not like how Manny Meskill does things, but I can't do anything about this. I don't set the rules. Reine is going to have additional time now with the theft of the jewelry. I'm sorry, but it was likely going to happen at some point today or tomorrow, anyway…" He thought he could hear his sister yelling in the background. This was likely why she'd been calling him. "Put Karen on. I'll talk to her, but she has to stand down and not interfere. What the hell is she doing there, anyway?"

"She said she's Reine's lawyer."

He wanted to bang his head against the steering wheel as he pulled up to a stop light. But instead he shook it. "Of course she is," he said, sarcasm dripping. "Put her on."

He heard his wife say something, likely to Karen.

"So you don't take my calls?" Karen said. There was the nastiness only she could give him.

"I'm working, Karen, investigating, doing my job. What the hell are you doing? Prison transport is there to take Reine back to prison. You're a lawyer. I shouldn't have to explain to you how it works when parole is revoked." He knew he sounded short, but he couldn't remember both his sisters ever fighting him and challenging him this way, butting heads with him, interfering with his job and position as sheriff. Worse, it felt as if his integrity were being questioned. Maybe that was what bothered him more than anything.

"Don't be an asshole, Marcus. Did you know they were coming to pick her up and take her back?"

He shook his head, knowing she couldn't see him, and let out a groan that sounded rough even to him, wanting to yell. Karen didn't go quietly into the night about anything. "No, Karen, I didn't know, but then, her parole officer doesn't run anything past me, nor does he have to, although it would be a professional courtesy. Manny Meskill isn't professional or courteous, but he is still her parole officer, who sets the rules she has to follow…"

"Marcus, she didn't do this." Karen could be a pit bull at times, and he could feel the punch coming right for him through the phone. "You have nothing but an accusation. If this were anyone else, she wouldn't be sitting behind bars right now. You would actually be looking for evidence and building a case first, getting your facts instead of taking the word of some guy."

"You're right, which is why an investigation is in full swing. But you should know I found the jewelry she took on consignment in a jewelry store. She was given an advance of a thousand dollars. Karen, no matter what you all think, I didn't want this to be true. But she did it. She stole the jewelry from a vulnerable old woman with dementia, and even though a bunch of people put her in a position she shouldn't have been in, her choice to take it was one hundred percent on her. She is responsible for her actions. You're her lawyer, so do your damn job. Get her to take responsibility for what she did, and then work some deal with the DA. That's how you can help her. But she is going back to prison, and there is nothing you or I can do about that. She made the choice. Now she has to deal with the repercussions. How many years she gets tacked on to her sentence is in your hands."

He heard the click of Karen hanging up on him as he pulled up in front of the Hirst house, where Therese's police cruiser was parked. "Unbelievable," he said in disbelief, feeling his tension rising. A blowout in his family was likely.

He turned off the engine and sat there for a second, seeing Eva's innocent face, anticipating the questions she was going to ask as soon as he walked through the door tonight. He didn't have a clue what to say that wouldn't bring a world of hurt to her.

"Damn you, Reine," he said as he gave his door a hard yank open, then reached for the plastic bag.

As he strode to the front steps, he took in the two-story house, the porch, and the garden bed, which was in bad need of weeding. Picturing Reine there just the day before, he lifted his hand and knocked on the white door. He could hear voices inside and footsteps as he turned around and took in the houses across the street, the quiet neighborhood.

The inside door opened, and there was his deputy, Therese. "Sheriff, Harold called, said you found the jewelry?"

He stepped inside the front entrance, with a small hall closet and a pony wall separating it from the kitchen. He heard voices as he closed the door, spotting the notepad she was holding.

"Yeah, right here. You get a photo and statement?" He held up the plastic bag of jewelry.

Therese nodded, holding up her notes. "Her daughter is digging out some old photos for me. She said she needed them for the insurance claim, anyway."

He followed Therese into the living room, which had a beige carpet, two green loveseats, and an easy chair where a woman with gray hair was sitting. An old TV tray beside her held a mug of what could have been tea or coffee, along with a glass of water, a newspaper, and a brown wooden box. She was looking right at him.

"Sheriff, this is Mrs. Hirst."

"Hi, Mrs. Hirst. I'm Sheriff Marcus O'Connell. How are you doing today?" He took in her light eyes, pale wrinkled skin, and confusion.

"Oh, hello, am I in trouble for something?"

"No, no, no, Mrs. Hirst, you're not in trouble. You had some jewelry that went missing, a ring, some earrings, and a brooch." He glanced over to Therese, who was looking right at him.

The old woman opened the wooden box on the TV stand, her hand shaking, revealing necklaces and rings crammed inside. "Could you help me put this on? My pearl necklace. My Herman gave it to me." She lifted the necklace out.

"No, Mom, you're not putting on the pearls again," said the daughter as she hurried back into the room, wearing white capris and a light blue sleeveless shirt that buttoned up in front. "Deputy, these are the photos I was sending to the insurance company," she said, handing them to Therese. Then she flicked her light blue eyes to him as she leaned down over the old woman, tucking her short dark hair behind her ears. She wasn't very tall. She took the pearls from the old woman and put them back in the box before closing it up.

"So do you need anything else?" she said. "You said that woman who was here yesterday is being charged? I can't believe they brought an ex-con right into my mother's house to look after her. And she was here alone with her. How can something like that happen?"

"Yes, ma'am, she is," Therese said. "Sheriff, this is Mrs. Hirst's daughter, Valerie. She's the one who called Better Way and reported the missing jewelry. She said when she came home yesterday, it was just Reine Colbert here with her mother…"

"As I said to Pete, who runs Better Way, it was because she'd never finished cleaning that I called to begin with. She was here for how many hours, and Ivy assured me the upstairs would be cleaned, the bathroom, my room, and the other rooms. She had plenty of time, but very little was done. I don't have time to look after my mother, which is a full-time job, as well as pick up the slack of someone I've hired to do the work. Apparently, she spent her time going through everything instead. I mean, what else did she take? There are a lot of valuable things in this house. What should I do, Sheriff, call you and add to the list as I figure out what else is gone? Then what?"

Marcus was still holding the bag of jewelry. He could hear in her voice how worked up she was, and he looked around the fully furnished home, which seemed overfilled with trinkets, art, cabinets, and stuff he couldn't imagine having. To him, it became clutter. He pulled in a breath. "Valerie Hirst, is it—or Donnelly?"

She made a face. "Donnelly is my married name. Well, I'm divorced."

Marcus nodded and held up the plastic bag. "So are these by any chance the items that were taken? The brooch, the ring, the ruby earrings?"

Therese hadn't shown him the photo, but he didn't need to see it from the way Valerie gasped, pressed her hand to her chest, and reached for the bag. "Yes. Where in heaven did you find them?"

Marcus didn't miss the outrage in her voice. "Unfortunately, I can't return them to you as of yet, as this is evidence. But I would like to talk to you about Lowes, the jewelry store where I found them. Were you by any chance in the store yesterday?"

She stared at him, still standing beside the old woman, who looked up at her. Her hand was on her mother's shoulder—protectively, it seemed.

"Valerie, what's going on?" Mrs. Hirst asked. Her daughter said nothing, just stared at Marcus.

"Just curious, Valerie," he continued, "considering that was where I found the items you said were stolen. The woman I spoke with at the jewelry store advanced someone by the name of Valerie Donnelly a thousand dollars on the consignment of this jewelry, which I understand is worth a lot of money. There's a surveillance camera, which my deputy is getting a warrant for right now, and I'm wondering who we're going to see on it: Reine Colbert, who was left here with your mother and accused of taking it, or you, Valerie? I have to say, description wise, you look similar to Reine—dark hair, same height, blue eyes."

The old woman was looking confused, and Therese had an odd expression. Marcus was ready to reach for his cuffs, feeling sick over Reine. He'd believed with everything inside him that she was guilty. But now he had a different feeling, and he knew he was right about this.

Valerie gestured to her mother. "I'm caring for a woman who barely knows who I am. Going into a jewelry store is not a crime. When I get a chance to get out of the house, I go to a lot of stores. I didn't realize I needed to report where I've been."

Marcus was still holding the bag of jewelry. "You accused a woman of stealing from you, stealing this, yet I found it in a jewelry store. We're getting the surveillance footage now, so are you telling me we'll see Reine Colbert? It's your name written in the consignment book."

She said nothing at first, still standing over the old woman, dragging her gaze from Marcus over to Therese. She lifted her hands. "I'm not saying I'm not on the surveillance footage in the store. As I said, I go into a lot of stores. I have a lot on my plate right now and can't remember everything I've done or everywhere I've been. It's a lot to keep track of."

She was nervous. He glanced once to Therese.

"Did you not tell me when I took your statement," Therese cut in, reading from her notes, "that you suspected Reine Colbert had stolen more of your things because she was an ex-con left alone in your house, so you immediately went to your mother's jewelry box because you had a feeling something was missing?"

Valerie was gripping her mother's shoulder. Just what the hell was this woman up to? "You found the jewelry," she said. "So if you return it, how about we just drop the charges? We have it back now. I would rather not pursue anything."

People backed into a corner would lie, spinning

stories that took on lives of their own. Marcus couldn't shake the feeling that Valerie Donnelly was hiding a lot of stories.

"Doesn't work that way," he said. "A woman was arrested and her parole revoked because you accused her of stealing."

"Sheriff, please. Misunderstandings happen. I've been known to overreact and forget I've done something. Again, I'm not pressing charges."

He shook his head and felt sick, staring at this woman, wondering if she had any idea what she'd done. "Misunderstandings? Reine Colbert, from what I understand, was left here to care for your mother alone when she was never supposed to be, and you accused her of going through your things, possibly stealing something else, and taking jewelry, this jewelry." He held up the bag again, because she was really pissing him off.

"Now, wait a second," she said. "When I called the nursing home, I was angry with Pete because the house was supposed to have been cleaned, and sometimes when I'm angry I say things and lash out. It's one of my faults. Again, I'm not pressing charges. I would like the jewelry back, please."

He dug his heels into the carpet, holding the bag she was seriously demanding he return to her. His hands were on the cuffs, and he really wanted to slap them on her, maybe because he'd done that same thing to Reine. And he hadn't believed her.

Valerie still hadn't admitted anything, but he knew deep down what she'd done.

"Right now, a young woman who was just getting her life back together, who was on parole, is on her way back to prison with additional pending charges against her because of you. You're saying it was the heat of the moment and you said things you didn't mean. But, Valerie, tell me right now, am I going to see you on that video, taking this jewelry into Lowes yesterday and putting it on consignment?"

Therese pulled out her cell phone beside him, lifted it, and took Valerie's photo. "We'll also be showing the jewelry store owner your photo," she said.

Valerie's face paled, and he could see the panic. "You know what? I'm not saying another thing. I think any more talking will be done through our family lawyer. I'm feeling particularly vulnerable, as if my words are being twisted, so I'm going to ask you to leave now."

He wanted to slap the cuffs on her and haul her down to the station, but he stared down at the old woman who looked to her daughter for everything. He knew Valerie wouldn't admit to the lie she'd spun. He'd have to have the evidence before he could do anything.

He gestured to Therese and took a step toward the door, then looked back at Valerie and the house, trying to get a picture of what was really going on. The feeling sickened him. "Call your lawyer, then, and tell him I want you both down at the station to give a statement today. Find someone to look after your mother, because if you don't, I'll come personally and bring you down myself."

His hand was on the door, and he pulled it open and walked out ahead of Therese, then pulled the door closed behind them.

"Sheriff, why are we not arresting her?" Therese said.

He pulled his hand over his face as he stood on the porch, then walked down the few steps, still carrying the bag of jewelry. "She didn't confess to anything. All I have is a name and security footage I haven't seen yet, which Harold better have a warrant for. But she's already spinning it. She made a mistake, was confused, overtired, stressed… At best, it's attempted insurance fraud, but it sounds as if it's just a bunch of accusations and nothing has been filed yet. A lot of people were quick to point the finger at Reine and believe the worst, including me.

"We'll talk to Pete, get his statement about what she said, exactly. But my gut tells me Valerie is likely selling off her mother's things, then maybe cashing in by reporting them stolen so she can make an insurance claim. I'd really like to see what claims have been filed and paid out by her insurance already, and her bank account. Also see if Valerie Donnelly has filed any crime reports in the past. Maybe she's done this before."

Therese didn't show much emotion, and he never knew what she was thinking, really. "So she gets away scot-free and Reine Colbert sits in jail."

He glanced at Therese and shook his head. "I didn't believe Reine. I arrested her based on an accusation from an employer and, yeah, on an assumption of guilt because she has a record and had an opportunity. Reine has had her parole revoked and is on her way back to prison. I would love to charge Ms. Donnelly in there instead. Then there's Pete from the homecare service, with the way he went off, and the nurse she was working under. It seems as if Reine didn't stand a chance. If anything, we'll be charging a bunch of misdemeanors, and lawyers will sweep it under the rug, whereas it's damn near impossible to un-ring the bell now that Reine has lost everything again. Dammit!"

"I'd have done the same as you, Sheriff, and arrested Reine," Therese said. "She's on parole. She doesn't get to walk around with the same freedom and liberties we do, and she doesn't get the benefit of the doubt."

Marcus looked back to the house, where Valerie was looking at him from the window. She had a phone to her ear, the curtain parted. He knew she'd walk and this would get filed away as a misunderstanding. "That doesn't make me feel any better about this situation, and it doesn't make it right. You took a statement from Valerie?"

"Yeah. Just need her to sign it." She held it up, her notes.

"Write it up, and then call in the nurse Reine worked with, the one who left her here alone. Call Pete too. I want to talk to each of them. Better yet, drive over to the Better Way office and pick up Pete and bring him in. I want a statement from everyone before they've had a chance to get their stories straight. I want them sitting in the same concrete room Reine sat in, getting a taste of how she felt."

"You got it, Sheriff. And what about Reine?"

He pulled open the door to his cruiser, breathing deeply, feeling the hurdles ahead. "Find a way to get her out," he said. Then he climbed into his car and pulled his cell phone from his pocket, dreading the next call he needed to make.

Chapter Eighteen

Bars clanged, voices echoed, and Reine held a folded blanket as her cell door closed. She knew she needed to pull her head from the horror of what she was living and instead focus on surviving life behind bars again. The same women were here, she knew, although she hadn't seen them yet, and the same guards had welcomed her back, but now there was the giant hole in her heart of having had her daughter ripped from her again.

Worse was Manny Meskill and the way he looked at her, talked to her. She knew whatever fate had in store for her, he'd see she didn't get a break. She put down the blanket on the thin mattress in her isolated cell, her legs sagging, remembering Karen, who'd fought and yelled and tried to stop Manny and the prison guards who had shackled her and transported her back to this place she now didn't think she'd ever be free of.

She heard the key in the lock, the steel door open, and turned to see the dark face of the guard, a large woman she'd always been wary of. Collins was her name. She was standing there, holding the waist chains. Reine remembered too well what had happened in the beginning every time she left her cell, being high risk. Apparently, she started back at square one.

"Your lawyer's here," Collins said. "Come on, you know the drill."

The guard shackled her wrists to the waist chain around her baggy jumpsuit, and her ankles were shackled too. She stood there stoically, because this was life behind bars. A hand gripped her arm, and she was escorted down the concrete hall, remembering her original charge and how the warden had told her this was what happened when she did what she'd done to a cop. High risk, her, Reine Colbert.

It was degrading now, and she said nothing because the ache inside her had left her numb. She wondered how long it would be before she earned privileges again, the freedom she'd earned there in prison before her dad's lawyer had finally won her release. Worse, she had no idea when the clock would start ticking again, counting down the time she had to serve. It could be worse this time, and she figured that was likely what Karen was there to tell her.

She stopped in front of the visiting room, and the guard unlocked the steel door. There was another guard inside, she saw as she shuffled in, taking in Karen, still pregnant, her hand on her stomach and alarm in her vivid blue eyes. She realized someone else was with her, Marcus, the sheriff himself, and she felt an anger burning inside her. She knew if the cuffs came off, she'd likely jump him, hit him, do anything to hurt him.

"Reine, I'm so sorry. Come and sit down. Please take those off," Karen said as the guard pulled her over to the metal chair and sat her down. All she could hear was the clang of chains, the guard's hand still on her. Reine had to look away, past the embarrassment and the hurt of being treated like an animal. Having Marcus there made the situation even worse.

Damn Karen for bringing him!

"No, can't happen," Collins said. "Orders of the warden."

Right, the warden who'd greeted her and looked at her with not an ounce of empathy. She'd never forget the coldness in her words as she'd said, "Welcome home. You'll wish you hadn't screwed up."

But then the hand was gone, and the door closed, and she took in the empathy she thought was in Karen's face. She dragged her gaze away because she couldn't not look at Marcus, whom she'd willingly given her daughter to and thought she would go to her grave hating. He stared down at her, his arms crossed.

"Are you here to grind me into the ground and tell me I'll never see my daughter again, how I screwed up and you'll make sure I spend a long time in here?" Reine said. She dragged her gaze over to Karen. "You brought him?" She knew she sounded accusing as she took in this woman she believed had cared and done the best for her. Now she wondered, for Karen, if this was more about protecting her family.

"Reine, that's not why Marcus is here. I wouldn't bring him to do that, and he wouldn't do it." Karen looked over to her brother, sounding as if she'd gone a round or two with him. "Marcus is here because he found the jewelry."

The knot twisted in her stomach, and all she could wonder was why, and how. "So is this where you tell me you can't do anything for me and that I'll never get out because of the theft?" She couldn't look at Marcus. She wished he'd leave.

"But you didn't take the jewelry," Karen said. Why did she appear so confused?

Reine didn't know why, but a laugh burst out, and she couldn't stop. Then she started crying, but she couldn't wipe the tears from her face as they spilled out. She shook her head at Karen, who appeared alarmed. "You think that matters?" she choked out. "I knew as soon as the accusation came out that it wouldn't matter. So where did you find it, hidden someplace in my suite? Tell me where it was planted. I know it won't matter, because anything I say, no one will believe me."

"I believe you, Reine."

Had Marcus really said that? She turned to the man who had put her there. She knew he couldn't have said that.

"Excuse me?"

Karen was looking at her brother in an odd way. Reine didn't understand what this was.

"It was found at a jewelry store, brought in yesterday on consignment," Karen said. "Apparently, from the description, it sounded like you, but the name on the register was Valerie Donnelly's."

Reine found herself dragging her gaze over to Marcus, realizing that was likely why he had the look he did on his face, the look of a lost puppy. Or was it shame?

"I had my deputy get a warrant for the surveillance camera," he said. "We paid a visit to the Hirsts, and imagine my surprise at how much Valerie resembles you, Reine. I don't even know where to begin in saying I'm sorry."

She pulled at her hands, but they didn't move from where they were shackled to the waist chain. Her nose was running, and she tried to move her face to wipe it on her arm, sniffing loudly. "Valerie, the old woman's daughter?" She looked from Marcus to Karen and back.

"I saw the surveillance myself," Marcus said. "Valerie took the jewelry in and put it on consignment. I have a statement now from the owner of the jewelry store. I've spoken with Pete again from Better Way Homecare, who said Valerie called him, accusing you of taking the jewelry, and he had no reason to believe she could be mistaken. The homecare nurse who shouldn't have left you said that was Pete's decision. He'd added an additional visit for her to handle, so he called her at the last minute and told her to leave you there to clean up. He said it was fine."

"It was fine?" she cut in, because it seemed she was damned if she did and damned if she didn't. "I told Ivy I wasn't supposed to be alone there, that I was supposed to go with her. My gut was screaming no, but I didn't argue because I needed to keep my job. You know the parole rules. I was also meant to work only until one thirty, but I was told not to cause a problem, to give extra, to work for free without complaining. The daughter was supposed to be back by two, but it was after four when she walked in. Meanwhile, I was dealing with her mother, who walked out the front door after breaking a pot in the kitchen. I couldn't do my job because there was an old woman there who couldn't look after herself, so I had to do it. And her daughter was stealing her jewelry, selling it? I was the perfect scapegoat. So when am I getting out of here?"

She saw the exchange between Karen and Marcus, the way he shut his eyes and breathed out, and her stomach knotted.

"You did charge her with theft, right?" she said. Why was it that Marcus didn't want to answer?

"No, I can't, because she has power of attorney for her mother and everything she owns. She's saying she forgot, and her lawyer said it was a misunderstanding."

Reine didn't think she'd heard right. She looked over at Karen, because here she was, having been classified as high risk and tossed back in a cell, and she hadn't done anything to deserve it. "This is a joke, right?"

Karen shook her head. "Unfortunately, it's not. But we're working on getting you out of here. We've gone to the DA about this, and even though charges won't be pressed against you for the theft, there is the matter of your revoked parole. The DA isn't too willing to un-ring that bell, saying the parole officer already indicated your refusal to follow the rules because you showed up on Marcus's doorstep. The system doesn't exactly work in your favor."

Reine shook her head and shut her eyes. She didn't want to hear any more, because she'd been down this road before. "No, no, no, you're saying I'm stuck here?"

Karen slapped the table in front of her. "You listen to me, Reine. It's political posturing because no one wants this to get out, not Better Way Homecare, who cut corners and let an ex-con stay alone with an elderly woman, and not your parole officer, who works for the state and would rather see you locked away than admit he screwed up and yanked your parole based on unfounded accusations. You'll have to go back before the parole board, but the state is already saying they will not allow all the circumstances of what transpired to be admitted in evidence, because the only thing they care about are the rules they set…"

"Yeah, I know, to stay away from the O'Connells," Reine said, cutting Karen off and putting all the venom she could into a glare at Marcus. "You have my daughter, and you just had to take it to my parole officer. Well, you got your wish, Marcus. I wish I'd never met you, yet now you have my daughter. The only thing I ever wanted was for Eva to be safe. Everything I did and have done is for her."

He leaned on the table, and she wished he would get the hell away from her. "I know, Reine. I don't know what to say other than that I'll find a way to fix this. We'll find a way to get you out of here."

She was nodding, but she didn't believe a word. She had enough anger to go around. "Sure, Marcus, I'll believe it when I see it. Ask yourself how easy it was for you to believe a lie. People who apparently matter more were automatically believed over me because I have a record, no rights."

"I know it's not fair, Reine…"

"You're kidding, right? When Eva and I were on the streets, I never realized we'd been put there by the class of people you're protecting. It seems they can say and do anything, create a lie about me and have it believed without even needing to prove it. There's something so fundamentally wrong here. I'm not a stupid woman, but I don't believe a word you say. Let's say you do manage to get me out and fix what you've caused. Where does that put me? Back to visiting a parole officer who'll be looking for another way to toss me back in here, another story about why he had to hit me. Then there's my daughter. I already know you expect me to just walk away and stay out of her life." She shook her head, not caring how bad he felt. "I hate you, Marcus O'Connell. Now please leave." She looked back at Karen. "And don't bring him back here. Are we done?"

She heard the door bang behind her.

"We're done here," was all Marcus said.

Karen walked over to her, her hand on her swollen belly. "Keep your head down. I'll get you out of here," she said. Then she was gone with her brother.

A guard reached for her arm and helped her up, and she allowed herself to be led back blindly to a tiny concrete cell, knowing she'd be there until the warden decided she wouldn't be. This time, when the image of her sweet daughter slipped into her head, she pushed it away.

Chapter Nineteen

arcus sat in his car in his driveway, trying to
make sense of everything that had happened,
from groveling to Karen and visiting Reine to meeting
with the lawyer who was the face of the Hirst family.

He knew his family was inside. He'd seen Jenny and
Alison walk into his house, and Owen and Tessa, and
even Luke and Chloe, but he'd ignored all of them.
Even when Charlotte had stepped out of the house and
gestured to him, he'd just looked away. He thought it
was Owen who had said something to her, encouraging
her to go back inside.

He didn't have a clue how to find the words to tell a
little girl why her mother, whom she'd seen just the day
before, couldn't visit her right now. He leaned back
against the headrest and shut his eyes.

There was a sharp tap on his window, and he looked
up to see Owen, who pulled open his door. Behind
them, Harold pulled up in his Kia with Suzanne and the
baby.

"You've been sitting out here almost half an hour. Karen filled us in," Owen said.

Marcus slid out, and Owen stepped back. He took in his big brother just as he heard the screen door to the house, and Luke and his dad stepped outside. He wondered how long it would be before Eva did, too.

"Yeah, well, how do I find the words to tell Eva why her mom is in prison again? And, worse, that it's my fault?"

Owen made a face, and the grimace said everything. Behind him, Harold passed the baby over to Suzanne, who he thought was likelier to shove a poker in his eye than have a civil conversation, and then Harold was walking his way.

"It's not all on you," Owen said. "Heard the woman stole her own mother's jewelry and tried to throw Reine under the bus."

Marcus shook his head. "Not entirely. She has power of attorney. As her lawyer argued, everything is going to her, and she needed the money because her mother's care is so expensive. Wasn't that what the lawyer said, Harold?"

At least he'd handled one thing right in this mess, letting Harold talk to the lawyer and to Pete, who'd turned out to be not just the manager but the founder of Better Way. Then there was the nurse who'd willingly put Reine in a position she couldn't defend herself from. He didn't know, out of all of them, who was more responsible or whether the blame was equal. Owen looked over to Harold.

"I spoke with Eileen, the ADA, who said she'll reach out to the parole board but told me not to hold my breath," he said. "She said rarely in this jurisdiction are changes in circumstance and new information heard. The conditions set forth have to do with you, Marcus."

He leaned his head back and shut his eyes, wishing he'd never gone to Manny. At the same time, the conditions of her parole should have been disclosed to him to begin with. What a mess this was.

"Karen's working on it?" Harold asked.

Marcus didn't know what to say. "Karen is almost eight months pregnant, and she's furious, which isn't good for her right now. I do know she's prepared to file every motion she can, not that it's going to do much good. Unfortunately, it'll come down to waiting for another opportunity with the parole board. Karen is furious with me, and I'm pretty sure Suzanne is about to take up where Karen left off, not that I can blame either."

Owen turned and glanced behind him, where Luke and their dad were talking on the porch, leaning on the railing. Maybe they knew he wanted some space.

"Marcus, you know you didn't have a choice," Harold said. "I would have done the same thing."

"Would you, really?" he said, nearly cutting off his deputy, who was his brother-in-law and a good friend.

"Yeah, I would have. You know that of everyone, I'm not going to tell you something because I think you want to hear it. You know damn well how it works. You have a property owner who calls in a theft, an ex-con who was there with the opportunity, and Reine in a desperate situation. She wanted her daughter back, which meant a lawyer, and where was she going to get the money? You had no control over what her parole officer did…"

"He hit her, abused her. God knows how many others he's done it to."

"And you can't prove that. It's her word against his, and in case you forgot, with his being a state employee, a parole officer with decades on the job, he's in a position of power and will always be given the benefit of the doubt without rock-solid evidence to prove otherwise. Therese did some digging, and he doesn't have a history of complaints against him. But the only thing that tells me is that he got away with it and intimidated everyone he did hurt. He must've threatened them, and they were smart enough to know they wouldn't win against him."

Owen pulled his arms across his chest and listened to the back and forth between Harold and him. When he heard a vehicle, he turned to see two black SUVs with the State of Montana logo. Of course, it was Jack, there because his wife was very pregnant and had been dragged into Marcus's mess.

"You know what? Give me a minute with Jack," was all Marcus said, reaching over and pressing his hand to Harold's arm. He walked around him toward his brother-in-law, who stepped out of the back seat of one black Tahoe, the door held open by a state trooper. He was in a dark suit, impeccably dressed as he always was.

Marcus crossed the grass over to him, nodding to the second approaching trooper. "Didn't expect you, but can't say I'm surprised," he said. "You picking up Karen?"

Jack didn't button his jacket. He said something to one of the troopers, who hung back as he closed the distance to Marcus. "If I don't, she'll camp out at the condo, and she's too far along. Heard it didn't go well."

"Depends," he said. "We had to watch Reine being

brought in by a guard, shackled like a high-risk offender. Apparently, the warden is sending her a message. I was embarrassed for her. She's back there now because of bureaucracy and a man who has the power to make her life hell. I know Karen is trying to work a miracle, but too much of this is my fault. I need to ask you a favor, Jack."

Jack said nothing at first as he stood there in front of him. There was something about him. Marcus never knew where he stood. "Well, you'd better ask, or are you just going to stand there?"

Marcus nodded. "I need you to grant Reine a pardon."

Jack was already shaking his head. "I am well aware of the circumstances, but I can't, as much as I want to. I have requests all the time on compassionate grounds, like where someone is serving time for something they didn't do, but because of some bureaucratic policy, they can't get out. The law isn't always right or fair."

Marcus didn't move, just pulled in a breath. He hadn't been able to stop thinking of Reine crying tears she hadn't been able to wipe away. He said, "Reine Colbert, once upon a time, lived in suburbia. She had a husband who was a firefighter, a hero who made a living helping others. They were happy, and they had Eva, but when she was just a baby, he got sick, really sick, with a type of cancer that killed him slowly. He struggled through treatments, but the insurance company came back and denied coverage, so all of a sudden, medical bills and treatments that should have been covered weren't. They cited a clause in the contract, saying they'd discovered he'd smoked when he was young. That was despite the doctors saying his being a firefighter was what had caused the cancer, breathing in the kinds of carcinogens he did. When he died, the hospital bills took everything else from Reine, her house, her job, her life, and then she and her little six-year-old girl were on the streets…"

"Save it, Marcus," Jack said. "I know the story of how Eva came to be yours, and I'm sympathetic, and I agree what happened wasn't fair, and it shouldn't have happened…"

"Then help me," he ground out. "I beg you, Jack. I don't want to go into my house and face my little girl and tell her that her mother is back in prison and I have no idea for how long, another year, two, five… Please, Jack, help me. I've never asked you for anything, but I am asking now. I'll do anything, you know that. You want me to get down on my knees right here in front of everyone? I will."

"For Christ's sake, Marcus, stop," Jack snapped.

Neither said anything for a moment, and Marcus could see the way Jack was struggling.

"You don't understand, Marcus. If I could grant her parole, I would do it in a second. But you already said it: She's Eva's mother, your Eva, who is technically my niece, my family. Abuse of authority is something the media will hit me with, and the opposition, and every other group out there…" He glanced away.

Marcus didn't know how to get through to him, how to convince him. But he knew this would scream a conflict of interest, abuse of his office, and become a nightmare for him.

"I know this is a big ask," he said.

Then Marcus heard the screen door open and saw Eva step out of the house, his mom behind her. He took in the haunted look in her eyes as she strode down the steps, over to him, and he prayed in that second that she'd forgive him.

Chapter Twenty

She stared at the concrete wall, lying on the thin mattress, when she heard a key in the door and sat up to see a different guard, Patty, with light hair and at least fifty pounds on her. Patty terrified her more than any of them. She wondered how many days had passed. She'd had no word on how long she'd be there.

"Come on," was all Patty said in that way of hers, never letting Reine know what she was walking into.

She stood up, expecting to be shackled again, but the woman only reached for her arm and pulled her out of the cell. She wondered for a minute whether she was going back into the general populace, whether the warden had figured she'd punished her enough.

"Where am I going? Do I finally get to use a phone? I'd like to call my dad."

"Keep walking," Patty said.

Phone privileges could take a while to earn, she knew. There were more doors, more buzzing. The noise was something she'd never gotten used to.

Suddenly, she was taken into a room she'd been in

before, and one of the other guards handed back her clothes.

"You're getting out," Patty said. Was someone messing with her? Patty gestured toward her. "Unless you love it here so much that you want to stay."

"How? I don't understand?" she said. Patty had walked back to the door, so she took in the other guard as she kicked off her prison shoes and set her fingers on the zipper of the jumpsuit.

"Was told the governor gave you a pardon," the guard said before turning around. "Lucky, I guess. Can't say I've seen that happen before."

Reine just stared for a moment, realizing the other guard had turned to give her some privacy. She pulled the zipper down and changed out of the prison jump-suit, then pulled on her old worn clothes and slid her bare feet into her shoes, still with a hole in the toe. She flicked her hand over her short dark hair, lifting it, and glanced back to the jumpsuit, praying she'd never have to wear it again.

"Pardon, how?" she said as she was escorted out into the hall once more, hearing the buzzing of the locks.

Another door opened, and then she was outside. For a moment, she blinked in the sunlight.

Karen. It had to have been Karen. She really had come through for her. She started walking, seeing the dirt and gravel of the parking lot, where a car was wait-ing. One foot in front of the other.

Then she saw her.

"Mommy!" Eva cried. She was standing near Marcus by the car, then running right for her, wearing blue jeans and a yellow and blue T-shirt, her hair in a ponytail. She was in her arms, and Reine went down on her knees. She didn't know who was crying, her or Eva or both, as she held her daughter and kissed her cheeks, her head, feeling the gravel dig into her knees as her daughter leaned down. She'd never felt anything so good.

She looked up and saw Marcus standing over them, wearing blue jeans and a faded T-shirt. Reine slowly got up, but she kept an arm around Eva, and he flicked his gaze down to Eva and then over to her.

"You okay?" he said in a low voice.

She glanced down to her daughter, who had her arms around her and was looking up at her with a smile. She nodded and said, "How? The guard said I was pardoned. I don't understand." She couldn't not touch her daughter. She was rubbing Eva's arm, not understanding how she and Marcus were there.

"Full pardon from the governor, so no parole. The slate is clean," he said, gesturing toward her.

She felt her brow knit. "So I'm free?"

"You're out, Mommy," Eva said, "and Marcus said you'll never have to go back, and you can come live with us."

She stared at her daughter, then lifted her gaze to Marcus. She wasn't sure she could get her tongue to move. Maybe it was the confusion on her face that had Marcus reaching over to run his hand over Eva's head. He looked at Reine.

"We had a family meeting," he said. "We want you to come and stay with us, with Charlotte and Eva and me. Charlotte and Eva have been working all morning, getting the place ready for you."

"Eva, can you go to the car?" Reine said. "I'll be right there. I just want to talk to Marcus for a minute."

When her daughter looked up at her, she didn't miss the hint of worry. Even as long as they'd been apart, she knew when she was scared, worried, or happy.

"Hey there, sweet pea, I told you it's going to be okay," Marcus said. "Let your mom and me talk, and then we're going home."

She only nodded before walking to the car, looking back once. Reine had to pull her arms over her chest, aching from everything she'd lost.

"So what the hell is this?" she said, unable to keep the nastiness from her voice. The way Marcus looked down at her and nodded, she didn't know what was coming, but her hands fisted, and the only reason she kept them by her sides and said nothing else was because Eva would be watching.

"This is me trying to make things right, Reine. Look, you're Eva's mother, but we adopted her, and I love that little girl as much as I love my son. We weren't just looking after her; she's our family. I know you blame me, not as much as I blame myself, but I don't want to be fighting with you over Eva, because it will tear her apart, and I can't have that."

She pulled in one breath, then another.

"We want you to move in with us," he said. "We have a room in the house for you."

It was absolutely absurd, and she wondered for a second whether there was a but coming. But he said nothing.

"So the pardon from the governor, Karen's husband, that was because of you?" she said.

He had the same vivid eyes as his sister. She remembered his siblings, all of them, and the way they'd stood together.

"You were owed it," he said.

For a moment, she felt so damn uncomfortable. She said, "I don't know if I can forgive you."

He nodded and gestured to his car, where her daughter was waiting.

"Eva really loves you," she said.

He looked down at her. "And we love her. So is that a yes?"

She made herself breathe. "For how long?"

He said nothing for a second. "You're Eva's mother, so that makes you part of our family, Reine." He gestured to her and said, "As long as you want."

Reine made herself nod, then started walking with Marcus to the car, thinking of her daughter and all the promises she'd made to her as she held her as a baby. "I'm still angry at you."

He kept walking with her, side by side. "I know, but that's the thing about family, Reine. Sometimes we do something that seems unforgivable, but in the end, we're family. That little girl over there, she deserves this. But just a heads up and a word of warning, my family, all of them, are waiting for us back at home."

She glanced up at Marcus, unsure what to make of the way he winced. "Oh, and should I be worried?" she asked as she strode to the passenger side. Eva fell in beside her and hugged her again.

"Only because they're nosy, and they'll intrude, but they care a lot," he said.

She glanced down at her daughter, who looked happier than she ever had. "Well, I guess I'm coming home with you."

Eva squealed and hugged her again, and when she looked over to Marcus O'Connell, she didn't miss the mist in his eyes or the smile he didn't try to hide. He opened his door, and Eva climbed into the back seat, and Reine sat in the passenger side.

As Marcus started the car, she pulled on her seatbelt, and there was a moment where she realized she couldn't stay angry with him.

She was with her daughter.

She was out of jail.

And, for the first time, she wasn't scared of what was in front of her.

Turn the page for a sneak peek of
THE GATEKEEPER
Available in print, eBook & coming soon to audio

The Gatekeeper

THE O'CONNELLS

**Seven years ago, she lost her husband.
Three years ago, her daughter was taken
from her.
Today, she's taking back her life.**

Being taken in by the O'Connells would be a bit overwhelming for some. But for Reine Colbert, the feeling of being on the outside, looking in is all too familiar. Yet when Suzanne O'Connell, the unruly rule-breaker, steps in with her very pregnant sister Karen to right all the wrongs Reine has suffered along the way, she exposes a deeply guarded secret involving crimes against other women, and the three soon find themselves in a perilous situation that could leave one of them paying the ultimate price.

The Gatekeeper

CHAPTER 1

R eine woke to the sun streaming in, and she stretched before jolting upright, taking a second to realize where she was. She pressed her hand over her heart.

The window by her bed was open, with a light breeze fluttering the white cotton curtains. The double bed was comfortable, and she took in the white walls, the white metal bedframe, the wicker dresser with a mirror and a chair in the corner, and a small closet. The floral comforter on the bed reminded her of spring. The room was so welcoming, and the way the morning light danced off the walls was comforting. She still had to remind herself this was real.

Reine pulled in a breath and swept back her bed hair as she looked over to the bedside table, which had a digital clock. For a moment, she felt the familiar panic that had her tossing back the comforter, sliding her legs over the edge of the bed, and standing barefoot on the soft cotton throw rug. The clock said nine thirty-two. Reine couldn't believe she'd slept so late.

She stumbled over to the mirror, taking in her image and the long light green pajama T-shirt and shorts, which hung loose on her. They had been sitting on the bed for her—from Charlotte, she thought. She reached for a light blue housecoat on a hook on the back of the closed bedroom door, something else she thought Charlotte had put there for her, and turned the knob.

Her heart hammered with unwelcome unease as she stepped out, hearing a woman's voice downstairs. It was so quiet, and she wondered if she would ever find her footing. As she walked down barefoot, the creak of the stairs halfway had her jumping and staring for a second at the closed front door, the one she'd been on the other side of a few days earlier. That seemed like another life-time now.

Reine pulled in one breath and then another, furious at herself for a second for being so jumpy. She forced herself to take another step down even though that irrational worry was still there, the worry that she could find herself thrown out the door and have her freedom yanked away again. She forced a swallow, willing her nerves to steady, as she heard the clatter of dishes and took in the short dark hair of a woman whose smile reached out to her.

"You're awake. Hope you slept well. Come on, sit. Coffee?" said Iris O'Connell, Marcus's mother, who had such a warm presence. Reine pulled out a stool at the island and sat beside two-year-old Cameron, who was in a high-back stool with a bowl of cereal and a cup of juice. He had dark hair with a natural wave, and she could see how much he looked like his father.

"I would love a coffee, thank you."

Iris filled a mug with big hearts on it. "Milk, sugar…?"

Reine shook her head. "Strong and straight, please."

Iris settled the steaming mug in front of her, and Reine lifted it, breathed in the coffee, which smelled heavenly, and took a swallow.

"This is good, thank you. Can't remember the last time I enjoyed a good cup of coffee." She glanced over to Cameron, who was staring at her, and back to Iris, who had her own mug of coffee and was now leaning on the island. "Eva's gone already, I guess. I wanted to be up and see her before she went to school." She didn't hear any other sounds in the house.

"You'll see her tonight. No one wanted to wake you. You had to be exhausted. Take some time, get some rest. Eva didn't want to go to school today; she wanted to stay home with you. Not sure how Marcus and Charlotte convinced her."

Reine took another swallow as she heard the front door open, and Suzanne walked in with her baby in a carrier.

"Hi, Reine…" she whispered. "I just got Arnie to sleep. He was fussy most of the night, up three times." She put the baby carrier right on the kitchen table behind her, and Reine took in the sleeping baby with a light blanket over him.

Suzanne walked right to the coffeepot and poured herself a coffee. "Harold had to work last night. Some call came in around two this morning. I'm sure it was the phone that woke the baby the second time right after I got him to sleep, so I took him to bed with me, and Harold never came home. He's going to be tired…" She had the fridge open and pulled out a plastic-covered plate of what she thought was leftover chicken from the night before, the barbecue.

This family seemed unusually close and so different in a way she didn't understand. She watched as Suzanne pulled out a piece and took a huge bite, and Iris only shook her head before taking the plate from her and putting it back in the fridge.

"Reine, how about some breakfast?" Iris said. "You have to be starving. I can whip you up some eggs and toast, or cereal…"

"Hey, and maybe Reine would like some leftover chicken? Not everyone eats cereal, Mom," Suzanne cut in after taking a big bite of meat from a thigh. She looked right at Reine. "I've never liked cereal. I'd just as soon heat up any leftovers from dinner in the fridge."

Iris shook her head and glanced up. Reine was really starting to get a picture of the dynamic of this family, Marcus and Charlotte's family, here in this house. She wondered when she wouldn't feel like an unwelcome guest.

"Eggs and toast, if it's not too much trouble," she said. Suzanne was still looking at her, unsmiling and unapologetic as she held that chicken thigh and chewed.

"It's no trouble at all, Reine," Iris said. "You live here now. You make yourself at home…" She moved Suzanne out of the way. There was something sweet about the teasing between them.

"That's right, because after today, you fend for yourself," Suzanne said. "I think we should put Reine in charge of side dishes for whatever Owen's barbecuing tonight. Did he seriously say tonight he wants fish?"

Reine didn't know what to say. She was stuck on the idea of her making a side dish. For what? She moved to lift her hand to ask, taking in the back and forth between mother and daughter, then pulled her hand down and decided to say nothing, trying to figure out what exactly they meant by "tonight."

"A friend of Owen's came back with a mess of trout, bull trout, or was it cutthroat?" Iris said to her before dragging her gaze back to Suzanne as if this were the most normal information to add to this odd conversation.

"Do you not remember the last time Owen barbecued cod, or was it salmon or something he picked up at the store? It was overcooked. He should stick to what he does best: burgers, chicken, or hotdogs. Or even pork chops. He hasn't done that in a while," Suzanne said before going on further about the fish.

Reine wondered whether they were talking about that night or a different night. She moved to raise her hand again.

"You have a lost look on your face over there, Reine. Everything okay?" Suzanne said. Meanwhile, Iris cracked eggs in a bowl before setting a fry pan on the stove and turning it on. Bread was in the toaster, as well.

"Well, I guess I don't understand," Reine said. "I'm supposed to come up with a side dish… Is this for a party? And Owen, your brother, is barbecuing? When? Is this at his place? I guess I don't understand what's going on. Maybe I'm just not clear on how everything works here. You look after Cameron? I take it Marcus and Charlotte are…"

Iris had poured the eggs from the bowl into the fry pan. Reine wasn't sure if that was an amused expression on her face.

Suzanne glanced her mother's way before looking

back to her. "Ah, I see you're trying to figure out how we all work. Well, we always have our noses in everyone's business. Family night happens…what, three of four times a week, usually? It's here, or at Ryan's, or at Mom's place, although with Tessa and Owen fixing up their little house and Chloe and Luke now living next door to them, I can see us starting to migrate more and more there. Harold and Arnie and I still live at his condo, which equals no house, no yard, and no barbecue." Suzanne took another bite of the chicken as Iris finished scrambling the eggs in the pan.

Reine was now starting to understand what Eva had said about family night. "So you basically have your own lives but are always together, and last night wasn't just because Marcus brought me back here?"

Suzanne was shaking her head as Iris scraped the eggs onto a plate and the toast popped up in the toaster. "Well, yeah, we were all waiting here to welcome you, but it's what we do. When she's in town, Mom looks after the kids, Cameron and Eva, either here or at her place, and when I get a job with the sheriff's department, Mom will also look after Arnie."

Iris rested the plate of eggs and buttered toast in front of Reine with a fork. "Here you go. Do you want peanut butter or jam on your toast?"

"Um, yeah, peanut butter would be great. Thank you. This is really nice…" She watched as Iris reached into the fridge and pulled out a jar of peanut butter, as well as a clean knife from a drawer, and slid them in front of her.

"Suzanne, you know Marcus already said no to a job at the sheriff's office," Iris said. "You really think you could work under him, considering the way you two butt heads? And do I need to remind you that your husband, Harold, is the lead deputy?"

Maybe it was hearing about the two men who'd arrested her that had Reine gripping the fork a little harder than she normally would have as she said, "Why do you want to be a cop?"

She hadn't meant to say it out loud. She glanced over to Cameron, who was eating with his hands now, picking the cereal out of his bowl, and she realized both women were staring at her. The moment had suddenly turned awkward.

"Well, for one, I loved being a first responder, but I got bounced out of that, and the current council here and the politics of the fire department have made sure I will never get hired here again. I think I would make a great cop, but Marcus keeps telling me no, he won't hire me."

Iris was looking at her as she slid her hand over the island. "You're still angry at Marcus?" she said. "I can see you're trying your best to hide the hurt. We could all see it last night, the tension that lingers between you and Marcus and Charlotte."

There it was, the eight-hundred-pound gorilla in the room, except neither was here. Yet she was under their roof, and she was still powerless even though she was free. "It doesn't go away overnight. I'm Eva's mother, but Marcus and Charlotte make all the decisions for her."

She hadn't meant to say that, either. After all, this was Marcus's family, closer than any she'd ever seen, and she was the outsider coming in.

"I understand, Reine, but know that you're welcome here," Iris said. "You're Eva's mother, and Eva is our family, and there is something about family, Reine. We fight, but we do forgive, eventually. You just need to find your footing. All I can say is just give it some time as you slip into this family. It's not all about their being in charge of Eva. It's about all of us. And Marcus feels horrible over what happened…"

"But I have no rights here." She wondered if she was smart or stupid for forcing her point. The awkwardness lingered again.

"You know what?" Suzanne said. "Finish up breakfast, and then get dressed. We're going out." She looked over to her mom. "Can you watch Arnie?"

She admired Suzanne and her determination. She wondered whether anything ever scared her.

"You know I will," Iris said.

"Okay, and where are we going?" Reine started as she reached for her fork again, feeling lost, not fitting in anywhere.

"It's a surprise, but it will do you good, give you a new perspective. Come on, finish up." Suzanne gestured at her plate, and Reine took in her bright smile.

Iris shrugged, looking back over to her. Just then, Cameron decided he was done, so Iris raced over and lifted Marcus's little boy, and Suzanne's baby started fussing from the car seat he was still in. Reine watched these two women she figured were trying to make her feel welcome. But, being the outsider, she still had no idea how she could fit into this family or what, exactly, her place was.

About the Author

"Lorhainne Eckhart is one of my go to authors when I want a guaranteed good book. So many twists and turns, but also so much love and such a strong sense of family."

(Lora W., Reviewer)

New York Times & USA Today bestseller Lorhainne Eckhart is best known for writing Raw Relatable Real Romance where "Morals and family are running themes." As one fan calls her, she is the "Queen of the family saga." (aherman) writing "the ups and downs of what goes on within a family but also with some suspense, angst and of course a bit of romance thrown in for good measure." Follow Lorhainne on Bookbub to receive alerts on New Releases and Sales and join her mailing list at LorhainneEckhart.com for her Monday Blog, all book news, giveaways and FREE reads. With over 120 books, audiobooks, and multiple series published and available at all, retailers now translated into six languages. She is a multiple recipient of the Readers' Favorite Award for Suspense and Romance, and lives in the Pacific Northwest on an island, is the mother of three, her oldest has autism and she is an advocate for never giving up on your dreams.

"Lorhainne Eckhart has this uncanny way of just hitting the spot every time with her books."

(Caroline L., Reviewer)

The O'Connells: The O'Connells of Livingston, Montana are not your typical family. A riveting collection of stories surrounding the ups and downs of what goes on within a family but also with some suspense, angst and of course a bit of romance thrown in for good measure. "I thought I loved the Friessens, but I absolutely adore the O'Connell's. Each and every book has different genres of stories, but the one thing in common is how she is able to wrap it around the family, which is the heart of each story." (C. Logue)

The Friessens: An emotional big family romance series, the Friessen family siblings find their relationships tested, lay their hearts on the line, and discover lasting love! "Lorhainne Eckhart is one of my go to authors when I want a guaranteed good book. So many twists and turns, but also so much love and such a strong sense of family." (Lora W., Reviewer)

The Parker Sisters: The Parker Sisters are a close-knit family, and like any other family they have their ups and downs. Eckhart has crafted another intense family drama… "The character development is outstanding, and the emotional investment is

high…" (Aherman,
Reviewer)

The McCabe Brothers: Join the five McCabe siblings on their journeys to the dark and dangerous side of love! An intense, exhilarating collection of romantic thrillers you won't want to miss. — "Eckhart has a new series that is definitely worth the read. The queen of the family saga started this series with a spin-off of her wildly successful Friessen series." From a Readers' Favorite award—winning author and "queen of the family saga" (Aherman)

Lorhainne loves to hear from her readers! You can connect with me at:
www.LorhainneEckhart.com
lorhainneeckhart.le@gmail.com

Also by Lorhainne Eckhart

The Outsider Series
The Forgotten Child (Brad and Emily)
A Baby and a Wedding *(An Outsider Series Short)*
Fallen Hero (Andy, Jed, and Diana)
The Search *(An Outsider Series Short)*
The Awakening (Andy and Laura)
Secrets (Jed and Diana)
Runaway (Andy and Laura)
Overdue *(An Outsider Series Short)*
The Unexpected Storm (Neil and Candy)
The Wedding (Neil and Candy)

The Friessens: A New Beginning
The Deadline (Andy and Laura)
The Price to Love (Neil and Candy)
A Different Kind of Love (Brad and Emily)
A Vow of Love, A Friessen Family Christmas

The Friessens
The Reunion
The Bloodline (Andy & Laura)
The Promise (Diana & Jed)
The Business Plan (Neil & Candy)
The Decision (Brad & Emily)
First Love (Katy)
Family First
Leave the Light On
In the Moment

In the Family
In the Silence
In the Charm
Unexpected Consequences
It Was Always You
The First Time I Saw You
Welcome to My Arms
Welcome to Boston
I'll Always Love You
Ground Rules
A Reason to Breathe
You Are My Everything
Anything For You
The Homecoming
Stay Away From My Daughter
The Bad Boy
A Place of Our Own
The Visitor
All About Devon
Long Past Dawn
How to Heal a Heart
Keep Me In Your Heart

The O'Connells
The Neighbor
The Third Call
The Secret Husband
The Quiet Day
The Commitment
The Missing Father
The Hometown Hero
Justice
The Family Secret

The Fallen O'Connell
The Return of the O'Connells
And The She Was Gone
The Stalker
The O'Connell Family Christmas
The Girl Next Door
Broken Promises
The Gatekeeper
The Hunted

The McCabe Brothers
Don't Stop Me (Vic)
Don't Catch Me (Chase)
Don't Run From Me (Aaron)
Don't Hide From Me (Luc)
Don't Leave Me (Claudia)
Out of Time

A Billy Jo McCabe Mystery
Nothing As it Seems
Hiding in Plain Sight
The Cold Case
The Trap
Above the Law
The Stranger at the Door
The Children
The Last Stand
The Charity
The Sacrifice

The Wilde Brothers
The One (Joe and Margaret)
The Honeymoon, A Wilde Brothers Short

Friendly Fire (Logan and Julia)
Not Quite Married, A Wilde Brothers Short
A Matter of Trust (Ben and Carrie)
The Reckoning, A Wilde Brothers Christmas
Traded (Jake)
Unforgiven (Samuel)
The Holiday Bride

Married in Montana
His Promise
Love's Promise
A Promise of Forever

The Parker Sisters
Thrill of the Chase
The Dating Game
Play Hard to Get
What We Can't Have
Go Your Own Way
A June Wedding

Kate & Walker
One Night
Edge of Night
Last Night

Walk the Right Road Series
The Choice
Lost and Found
Merkaba
Bounty
Blown Away: The Final Chapter

The Saved Series
Saved
Vanished
Captured

Single Titles
He Came Back
Loving Christine

For my German Readers
Die Außenseiter-Reihe
Der Vergessene Junge
Der Gefallene Held

For my French Readers
L'ENFANT OUBLIÉ